CHAPTER ONE

The wisest plan would be to return to the hospital—Helen knew that. Matron had said there would always be a job for her at St. Christopher's. 'If you want to return when your mother is better, you have only to let me know.'

Then why didn't she? Because the hospital was associated with the memory of David and would, therefore, be too constant a reminder of a man who had turned his back upon her, a man she would never see again?

The shrill insistence of the telephone cut into Helen's thoughts, recalling her to the present. A man's voice echoed down the line and in the tired recesses of her mind it struck a familiar chord.

'Helen—is that you? This is Paul—Paul Brent.'

'*Paul!*' She laughed a little, partly with pleasure and partly with astonishment. 'I thought you were in Buenos Aires—or in the middle of the Atlantic!'

'We docked at Southampton last night. I knew nothing of your mother's death until some belated newspapers came aboard and I chanced on the obituary column. My dear, I really am sorry. I know how devoted to her you were . . .'

1

'Thank you, Paul.'

'You'll be going back to St. Christopher's, I suppose?'

'I don't know. I haven't yet decided what I shall do.'

'I could make suggestions. One, at any rate. But for the present I'll take you out to dinner and promise not to propose until we reach the coffee stage!'

The old, light-hearted note had crept back into his voice. It could never be absent for long, and Helen was glad of it now. She had always been fond of Paul. Fond, but nothing more. That was why he took the job of ship's doctor on the *Carrioca*, gaily promising not to jump overboard in mid-ocean—but making her feel a little guilty, nevertheless.

She had wished many times that she could love him. It would be so much more sensible than carrying a torch for a man who didn't care for her, a man who could turn his back upon her and walk out of her life, leaving a gap which had never been filled . . .

'Helen—are you there?'

'Yes—yes, I'm here—'

'Then be ready for a tall, handsome sailor at seven o'clock to-night. And give him a good welcome!'

'I will,' she laughed, and rang off.

The atmosphere of the room seemed to have lightened, and her heart with it. During these past weeks she had forgotten how to be

SISTER AT SEA

Rona Randall

CHIVERS

THORNDIKE

This Large Print edition is published by BBC Audiobooks Ltd, Bath, England and by Thorndike Press®, Waterville, Maine, USA.

Published in 2004 in the U.K. by arrangement with Juliet Burton Literary Agency.

Published in 2004 in the U.S. by arrangement with Juliet Burton Literary Agency.

U.K. Hardcover ISBN 0–7540–7708–X (Chivers Large Print)
U.K. Softcover   ISBN 0–7540–7709–8 (Camden Large Print)
U.S. Softcover   ISBN 0–7862–5971–X (Nightingale)

The text of this Large Print edition is unabridged.
Other aspects of the book may vary from the original edition.

Set in 16 pt. New Times Roman.

Printed in Great Britain on acid-free paper.

British Library Cataloguing in Publication Data available

Library of Congress Cataloging-in-Publication Data

Randall, Rona, 1911–
    Sister at sea / Rona Randall.
       p.   cm.
    ISBN 0–7862–5971–X (lg. print : sc : alk. paper)
    1. Nurses—Fiction. 2. Physicians—Fiction. 3. Ocean travel—
    Fiction. 4. Motion picture actors and actresses—Fiction.
    5. Triangles (Interpersonal relations)—Fiction. 6. Large type
    books. I. Title.
    PR6035.A58S57 2004
    823'.912—dc22   2003061637

light-hearted.

She was ready for Paul at seven. She wore a dress of grey silk jersey and he regarded her with approval. 'That frock,' he said, 'clings in all the right places . . .'

He took her to La Cucaracha, mistakenly believing that the best way to cheer a person was to give them lots of music and crowds of people. Actually, it wasn't Helen's kind of place at all, but because she knew why he had chosen it she smiled her appreciation. And the food was good. Very good. So was the Latin-American music, beating out insistently, but a little mercilessly. She tried hard to appreciate it, but towards the end of the meal Paul said, 'You're not liking it much, are you?'

'I'm a little tired, that's all.'

'What a clot I am! I thought music and colour might help. Not only you, but me. I wanted to avoid soft lights and sentiment, sternly telling myself to wait for the time and the hour. And now I find I can't. I want to talk to you seriously. And not as a brother. I'd hate to think that was how you regarded me.'

But it was. Even when he had taken her to hospital dances, openly proud and admiring, she had felt nothing but a gentle affection for him. A grateful affection, for he had come to the hospital very shortly after David had left, just when she needed a friend. But he never knew of the part David Henderson had played in her life.

3

And, of course, she had never any proof that David's interest in her was anything more than professional. Nothing to go on, but a fleeting glance, a sudden awareness. Their outings together had been merely relaxation after long sessions on duty—dinner in some quiet restaurant, or a visit to a theatre; even, occasionally, dancing somewhere, when his arm would hold her closely and his cheek brush hers. But that was all. And what did it add up to? Unspoken declarations which existed only in her imagination? It seemed so, for his parting letter had been polite, but final.

So it was about time she put all thought of David Henderson out of her head for ever. All the same, she didn't want Paul to become serious. Not to-night. Not just now.

He sensed her withdrawal and said gently, 'You're tired. You've just come through a hard time, haven't you?'

'Losing one's parents is always hard, although I don't remember my father's death—he was killed at the outbreak of the war. I was quite small, and before that he travelled such a lot I rarely saw him.'

'What did he do, your father?'

'He was a zoologist. He travelled about the world collecting rare animals.'

'Haven't you ever wanted to travel, as he did?'

'Often—and intensely.'

And particularly since her mother's death.

4

Helen had become conscious of an urgent desire to dig up her roots; spread her wings; start to live. But how could she do that? Her savings were meagre and her mother's estate negligible. There would be no money to squander, so, obviously, the best thing was to return to St. Christopher's and continue where she left off. And be grateful.

'Tell me about the *Carrioca*,' she said, changing the subject abruptly.

'She's a nice vessel. Twenty-six thousand tons of luxury.'

'You like being a ship's doctor?'

'With reservations.'

She wanted to ask what those reservations were, but refrained. She was still a little wary, afraid of leading up to the point of provocation between them. Paul had quit his houseman's job at St. Christopher's, which he had held for only a year, when she rejected him. That was more than twelve months ago, but it had left her with an odd sense of responsibility towards him. But for her, he would have remained. He might have gone far. He wasn't a doctor of brilliant promise, but he was a conscientious one.

'Tell me about your life at sea,' she demanded, and he talked about Salvador and Rio, Santos and Montevideo; about Buenos Aires, too. She sat enthralled.

'You're bad for me, Paul. I almost wish you hadn't turned up again!'

5

'Why?' he asked, adding with a grin, 'Do I disturb you, Nurse? I hope so.'

She laughed.

'Only with envy. I'd give anything to see the world . . .'

'Then marry me and you can. The wife of a ship's doctor on the Imperial Line gets a passage at reduced fare. Personally, I'd pay the lot to have you with me.'

He meant it, too.

She said gently, 'I wouldn't marry you just for that reason, Paul.'

'Marry me for any reason! I don't care what it is, so long as you do.'

'You'd mind very much—afterwards.'

'I love you, Helen. I've never stopped loving you. Now you've lost your mother I can see no reason for not marrying me. She was your reason for turning me down, wasn't she?'

So that was the interpretation he had put upon her refusal! Well, perhaps it was a good thing. Perhaps the thought had been a buffer between himself and pain. But now the buffer was removed, what would he expect? Capitulation. That was why he had got in touch with her again, after months of silence.

She was touched by his loyalty and devotion, and suddenly that feeling of responsibility towards him, that sense of obligation, came flooding back.

When she made no reply Paul said, 'Never mind. I'll be round in the morning to talk some sense into you.'

'Please don't, Paul—'

'Don't you want to see me?'

'Yes—but don't—don't rush me—'

'I couldn't rush you twelve months ago but I won't give up trying. In any event, you're not going back to St. Christopher's, *that's* for sure!'

'It's the most sensible thing to do. Besides, what alternative is there?

'Other than marrying me, you mean?' He laughed, and dropped a light kiss upon her cheek, but there was a tenseness about him which didn't deceive her. He wanted much more than a light kiss from her. 'I have an idea,' he said, 'but there's a bit of spade-work to be done. I'll get on to it first thing in the morning.'

CHAPTER TWO

Helen awakened feeling extraordinarily refreshed. She had slept long, and late—deep relaxed sleep which she hadn't experienced for weeks. She bathed, then slipped into a white towelling robe and pattered into the kitchen to make coffee and toast. To her horror, she saw that it was eleven o'clock. She was just finishing breakfast when the front-door bell rang.

It was Paul, looking tall and handsome and,

7

suddenly very dear. 'You've caught me napping —almost!' she laughed. 'I've only just tumbled out of bed!'

'Then tumble into some clothes. You have an appointment in less than an hour. I'll give you fifteen minutes to get ready, Helen. It will take us longer than that to get to Fenchurch Street.'

'Fenchurch Street? Why are we going there?'

'To see if we can get you signed on as ship's nurse on the *Carrioca*.'

'*Paul!*'

'Doesn't the idea appeal? You said you wanted to see the world. Well, the *Carrioca* will show you a portion of it, with me as escort.' He laughed at the sight of her incredulous face. 'I thought of it last night. The ship turns around in a week and I want to keep you under my eye. The girl who was nurse on the last voyage left to get married and, so far, hasn't been replaced. So I rang the Medical Personnel Officer first thing this morning, recommending you highly, and you're to attend for an interview at twelve-thirty. Hence the urgency. Can you get ready in fifteen—' he glanced at his watch. 'No—twelve minutes?'

She ran into the bedroom, calling over her shoulder, 'I used to do it in five, when I was late for duty!'

She was ready in ten minutes flat, looking

8

immaculate in a dark suit with touches of white. She wore a small, head-hugging hat, and her smooth blonde hair was braided in the nape of her neck.

Paul's glance spoke volumes.

'You'll do, Helen. *More* than do. If the M.O. doesn't jump at you I'll eat that ravishing little hat!'

It wasn't the hat which landed her the job, but her qualifications, and the next few days passed in a whirl of preparation. Helen's life changed abruptly, carrying her along on a mounting tide of excitment.

'I'm living in a dream, Paul! I'm only afraid that I'll wake up at any moment.'

'If you do, it will be on board the *Carrioca*, with me standing beside you.'

*   *   *

The night before sailing Paul said suddenly, 'Marry me, Helen. Marry me now. There's nothing to come between us anymore . . .' She hesitated. He was so very kind and sweet and—there were different kinds of love, weren't there? Different degrees and intensities. She could never love Paul in the way she had loved David, but perhaps the feeling she had far him was none the worse for that.

Paul asked gently, 'Why do you hesitate?'

'Because I'm not sure that what I feel for

9

you is enough . . .'

'It is enough for me. You love me, Helen—I'm sure of that. You hesitate because you're stunned by your mother's death and bewildered because you find yourself alone for the first time in your life. But you're not alone. You have me. And now there's nothing to stop us from marrying.'

'Except the shipping line. They stipulated that the job was for a single girl.'

Paul gave his infectious chuckle.

'Well, you were single when you applied for it. You're single now. But you don't have to remain so. We could be secretly engaged and get married at the end of the voyage. By that time the line will be so anxious not to lose you it will waive formalities.'

She felt as if she were upon the brink of a precipice, but an inviting one. And Paul's hand was there to help her over—a comforting and welcoming hand. She looked at his frank face and a wave of tenderness swept through her. Impulsively, she held out her hands.

Was it a gesture of acceptance, or gratitude? Even in her own mind, she was uncertain. But Paul wasn't. His face flushed with happiness.

'You'll never regret it, Helen, I promise you that. Oh, my darling, I've waited so long.'

'Little more than a year,' she prompted.

'So you know precisely how long I've been away! That proves you love me!'

Later, when she was alone, she was aware of

10

a deep sense of peace. She'd been honest with Paul, and he had agreed to accept whatever degree of love she could offer. 'I'll see that it grows deeper and stronger every day,' he had assured her confidently, and she had clung to him, closing her eyes with a sigh of contentment.

No, she didn't regret what she had done. Paul was a fine man, a good man, and he meant a lot to her. He had brought reality and hope into her life, and that was better than cherishing memories and a secret hurt. A girl couldn't live on memories. She should turn her face to the future.

'I'll be a good wife to Paul,' she vowed, and thought of him with tenderness.

Before going to bed she stood for a moment looking at her half-packed suitcase. Her uniforms and other clothes had already gone to the dock—in the morning all she had to pack was her night attire and after that she would walk out of the flat to a new and exciting future. She would never be lonely again. She would never again lie awake in the dark reaches of the night, thinking of a man to whom she meant nothing. Remembering, remembering, remembering . . .

But could one switch memory on and off at will? Could one control or regulate it? I must she thought frantically, and was aware of a sudden acceleration of fear. At all costs she had to forget the past, for now she was engaged to Paul. How it had come about she could scarcely remember, but at some point in the evening she had said yes.

And she knew she had done the wisest thing, that she was lucky to have the love of such a man.

As if summoned by the power of thought, the telephone rang, bringing Paul's voice across the shadowy rooftops, through the night air, right into her heart. 'I had to say good night again,' he said softly. 'I had to hear your voice . . .'

A quiet happiness ran through her and when she replaced the receiver fear had slipped away into the shadows.

She switched off her bedside lamp and lay in the darkness with her hands clasped behind her head, too excited to sleep. To-morrow, at ten-fifteen, she would catch the boat train from Waterloo and once aboard the *Carrioca* Paul would be with her almost constantly . . . They would work together, dine together, go ashore in distant ports. Oh, she was lucky beyond her wildest dreams!

Dreams! she thought, impatiently. I have lived with them for too long. They have borne me company ever since David walked out of my life.

Her thoughts went winging back to that first meeting with him. She had waited, expectantly in her little office beside the children's ward, wondering what the new consultant would be like, and her first reaction had been one of surprise, for he was young—a man in his early thirties, far from handsome, with an intent serious face which creased into an endearing smile when confronted by his small patients. With the staff he smiled very little. They only saw the professional side of him and it was a long time before she, Sister Cooper of the children's ward, was allowed to glimpse his personal side at all.

It happened unexpectedly, after a long and anxious session with a small patient whose life was touch and go. David had pulled the child through and when the anxiety was over, Helen had gone out of her way to congratulate him.

His smile had been warm and grateful.

'But you continue where I leave off, Sister. The child is in your hands now, and I couldn't wish for better.' The unexpected praise had brought a flush to her cheek, and he had looked at her intently for a moment, then said, 'We're both tired—and hungry. How about a bite to eat?'

And that was the beginning. After that there were other evenings, other outings. Sometimes he would forget himself in work for weeks, then emerge like a man released from a spell. Medicine was his life and any woman, she knew, would be secondary to it. That was why it seemed so incredible that he should give it all up because of one failure . . .

Helen shivered. The night was suddenly

cold. She went to the kitchen to heat some milk, but still could not relax. She was back in the past again, seeing the white faces of Christine Derwent's parents as they heard that the drug David had sought their permission to use, had failed.

But he hadn't guaranteed success. That was why he had asked for their consent. Meningitis had been followed by complications which had responded to no known remedy, and for weeks David had fought, working ceaselessly, going without sleep, searching and experimenting to find the answer. And he had found one which offered a fifty-fifty chance. 'Providing,' he said, 'that the parents will agree.'

And it was because the parents had agreed that David was exonerated when they brought their charge of negligence before the Medical Council—for Christine, a promising little ballet dancer for whom a great future was predicted, unexpectedly and unbelievably lost the use of her legs. The meningitis was cured, but the child could never walk, let alone dance, again.

All the heartbreak of those days came swirling back through the shadows of the night, clutching at Helen's memory with merciless fingers. Once again she stood before the Court of Inquiry, saying more than her party piece in David's defence, aware of his tense face staring straight ahead as he sat before the panel of judges.

14

'Doctor Henderson never predicted success —that was why he asked the parents' consent before using the drug. I'm certain the child couldn't have been in better hands and that he actually saved her life!'

She had said a lot more than that—more than she had meant to say, more than she had been advised to say. But it had to be spoken, it had to be declared. And he was exonerated by the British Medical Association, and rightly.

But David was a sensitive man with high ideals. He blamed himself bitterly, resigned from the hospital, and sent Helen a courteous letter of thanks—and farewell.

She had never been able to destroy that letter. It was her only link with a man who meant a lot to her—a man who, she had once believed, had cared for her. How mistaken she had been! She was so unimportant to him that he had been able to turn upon his heel and forget her.

Resolutely, Helen took from the bottom of her suitcase a small, old-fashioned box. As a child it had contained some long-forgotten toy, subsequently becoming a receptacle for her most treasured possessions; snapshots of her parents, newspaper cuttings about her father, her nursing certificates—and the letter David Henderson had written to her after the hearing. Now she took it out and read it slowly,

'*My dear Helen,*

'*I want to thank you for your loyalty, not only at the hearing this afternoon, but throughout the months we have worked together at St. Christopher's.*

'*I am resigning from the hospital, giving up Medicine and going away to think things out. I have failed in a job which meant much to me.*

'*You spoke up valiantly to-day, but all your excuses cannot alter the fact that I am responsible for what happened to that child. So it is better that I resign. I don't know, yet, what I shall do.*

'*Thank you for everything.*

'*David.'*

From that day to this, she had heard nothing of him, but she had always believed that one day his treatment of Christine Derwent would be proved right. She still believed that. But she had to destroy the memory of him, for her own sake.

Swiftly, she tore the letter into shreds, then dropped them into an ash-tray, set alight to them and watched tongues of flame obliterate his strong handwriting. Nothing was left but a heap of blackened ash.

She felt a sudden sense of release. For too long she had clung to a memory which had no substance. How long had *he* remembered *her*? No time at all, if it was as easy as that to walk

16

out of her life. He must have known that she would have stood by him, whatever he wanted to do.

But not now. He belonged to the past, to things discarded. She would never see him again.

Nor would she think of him again, now that she had agreed to marry Paul.

CHAPTER THREE

The hours before sailing were a whirl of activity. Helen was busy in the surgery, helping Paul to inoculate new members of the crew. She herself had been inoculated against tropical diseases before coming aboard, but, Paul told her, there was always a long line of engineers, stewards, deck-hands and others who just didn't take the trouble until checked up on. Precautions were taken against all major infections, although there was always the risk of mild fevers or malarias.

But at length she had prepared her last hypodermic, sterilised it, and put it away.

'Like to go up on deck?' Paul asked. 'Watching the ship up-anchor is always interesting.'

A few minutes later she was standing beside him at the ship's rail, seeing the dockside gradually recede as the competent busy little tugs manoeuvred the *Carrioca* from her moorings, like a pilot fish towing a whale.

'I don't know *how* they do it!' she marvelled.

'Years of experience, my dear,' said a fatherly voice, and Helen turned to see the kindly face of Joseph Burton, Chief Purser, regarding her with a smile. He was a weather-beaten, burly man, known to everyone as Uncle Joe. His eyes twinkled benignly behind old-fashioned, steel-rimmed spectacles.

'Years of experience, and years of skill,' he added, 'and if I tried my hand for half a century I'd never master it.'

He smiled upon them, thinking what a good-looking couple they were—a credit to the Imperial Line, without a doubt. Doctor Brent wore his uniform well and so, for that matter, did Sister Cooper, although it seemed a pity to hide so pretty a figure beneath so much starch.

He hoped she'd have a, chance to display it in the ship's pool when they reached warmer parts. Uncle Joe appreciated a good figure, although, to his way of thinking, modern ones were too flat. Like ironing boards.

'Settled in your quarters yet, Sister? Comfortable, I hope?'

'I shall be more comfortable when I've had a chance to unpack. I've scarcely had a moment a breathe since I came aboard!'

The two men laughed and Paul said, ' Don't worry—that was only the first rush. There'll be

18

a lull until passengers get settled in, then some will remember they are bad sailors and start ringing for us. But not until they've explored the ship, made their dining-room reservations, fought over the best positions for deck chairs, studied the passenger list, and decided with whom they want to scrape acquaintance. Until then, you can enjoy a brief respite so make the most of it.'

With me, said his eyes, but only Helen saw that. Uncle Joe was too busy studying the new ship's nurse and deciding that he liked the look of her very much. She reminded him of his eldest daughter back home. He hoped she would stay with the *Carrioca*. Too many nurses regarded a luxury liner as a hunting ground for husbands—preferably rich. The last one had annexed a wealthy Brazilian coffee planter and hopped off to London to marry him before he changed his mind and sailed back to South America without her. Amongst the crew, the odds on her success had been high.

This one, he thought, looked very young to hold the qualifications he had seen on her papers, so she must be a worker, good at her job, and the *Carrioca* was lucky to get her.

'Any interesting passengers aboard, Purser?'

It was Paul who asked, not because he was particularly interested with Helen aboard, but simply to make conversation. Obviously, Uncle Joe was in no hurry to get back to his office. Like them, he had come up for a breather

19

after the preliminary rush.

'The usual lot. Business tycoons, government officials, industrialists on expense accounts, and rich old globe trotters. And a film unit this time. I hope they won't give my staff too many headaches. They're off to Buenos Aires on location.'

'What's the film?' Paul asked.

'*Strange Destiny*, I believe it's called, from some book or other. Don't know it. Not a great reader myself.'

'Nor I,' admitted Paul.

Helen, who was, said, 'It was this year's best-seller, and I'm not surprised. It was wonderfully written by an entirely unknown author.'

In fact, the book had completely absorbed her. There was something about the way it was written which had held her from the start.

'It will make a wonderful film,' she continued, ' but why Buenos Aires? The story is about a provincial doctor in the heart of industrial England!'

'Film-maker's licence, I suppose,' said Uncle Joe. 'No doubt South America presents a more romantic background for Lola Montgomery. She's the star. It'll give the crew a thrill to have her aboard, I dare say. Quite a smasher, I believe.'

'And is *she* a member of the cast?' Helen asked, indicating an extremely pretty girl talking to a nearby deck steward, who was

20

placing her chair in a sheltered spot. She was young—very young—and dark. Her olive skin had a pale amber tone which was reflected in her maize-coloured travelling coat. A beautiful coat, Helen thought appreciatively— a beautiful price, too, no doubt. But everything about this girl was beautiful, including the expression upon her face, which was one of such natural sweetness that Helen's heart warmed to her.

'Whoever she is, she's one of the prettiest girls I have ever seen, and part of her charm is that she's quite unselfconscious . . .'

Paul said she looked a nice kid to him. 'One of the film unit?' he asked Uncle Joe.

'Dear me, no—I can't see Pedro Cortez allowing his daughter to go on the films!'

'Cortez, the South American millionaire?'

'None other. She's his youngest daughter— Belita—on her way home from finishing school in Europe. I've instructions to keep an eye on her, she's travelling alone, so I'd better start by seeing if she has all she wants.'

Uncle Joe saluted and was gone.

'Thank goodness,' said Paul. 'I was beginning to think I would never have you to myself. Do you realise I've been unable to kiss you since we came aboard? The devil of it is that I can't now, in full view of the promenade deck!'

'I must go below and unpack.'

Reluctant as she was to leave the wide,

clean deck the thought of settling into her attractive quarters was pleasurable. Helen had expected nothing so luxurious as her own shower-room, nor a cabin furnished with an eye to beauty and comfort. There were panelled walls of pale duck-egg blue, chintz curtains and upholstery, a writing desk which concealed a neat dressing-table, and easy-chairs in which to relax and entertain friends. And lots of drawers and cupboard space. In fact, her quarters were as skilfully designed as the ship's surgery, which had impressed her at a first glance.

They were walking towards the companion way when piercing scream sounded above the deep throb of ship's engines. A child's scream, petulant with rage. And suddenly the child herself appeared, racing along the deck with a harassed, dowdy woman hard on her heels.

'I won't, I won't, *I won't*!' stormed the child—a little girl of about seven, elaborately over-dressed.

'Wow!' murmured Paul. 'Whose little virago is that, I wonder?'

The child, caught by her agitated pursuer, turned upon the woman and shouted, 'If you so much as *touch* me, I'll bite!'

The woman retreated as if already bitten, but summoned courage to protest, 'Now, Carol dear, you mustn't be naughty! I'm sure your mother wouldn't like it.'

'Huh! She wouldn't even care! She does as

she likes, so why shouldn't I? When I grow up I'm going to be a film star, too, and then I won't share a cabin with *anyone*. I'll have a suite to myself, like Mummy's.'

The woman fluttered helplessly. She was obviously incapable of dealing with such a child.

'And what is wrong with the cabin you've got?' Helen asked calmly.

The little girl wheeled round, eyed Helen with brief defiance, sensed the disciplined authority behind the nurse's smile, and subsided.

'Who're you?' she asked sullenly.

'Sister Cooper—and this is Doctor Brent. Is anything wrong? Can I help?'

Her glance travelled to the harassed woman, who fluttered nervous hands and sighed, 'She refuses to to share a cabin with me—and she must, of course, because her mother booked it—'

'She did not!' the child stormed. 'The film company made all the reservations—*that* I know!'

'But your mother employed me to look after you, dear . . .'

'That doesn't mean sleeping in the same room. I'll bet you snore. I'll bet you snore like a trumpet. I *won't* share a cabin with you. I want one to myself.'

'If your mother agrees—'

'She will. She lets me have anything I want!'

23

'Better find out if there are any single cabins left,' Paul put in sensibly.

'*And* take a look at them,' Helen added. 'They're all below decks. I take it your double one is up here, on Promenade.'

'Of course it is! How could anyone sleep deep down in the ship?'

'Lots do. Come and see how you like it. It's dark, of course—lights on all the time—and the inside cabins have no portholes.'

'I don't believe it!' said Carol, clinging to her defiance. 'How could any fresh air get in?'

'Ventilation. Air conditioning. They're cool and airy, but small, of course. After a cabin on promenade deck, you'd feel rather cramped, and you'd be a long way from your mother. I expect she has a state-room on this deck, hasn't she?'

'Of course! She's *Lola Montgomery*!'

So this was the child there'd been all the fuss about both parents fighting for her custody when the sensational divorce went through. Lola Montgomery's private life was never private—either she saw to that, or the publicity boys did. Whichever way it was, the whole world knew she had just separated from her wealthy steel-magnate husband after eight years of a rackety marriage. The tension, the quarrels, the bickering, coupled with over indulgence of the child, had obviously had adverse effects upon Carol. Helen experienced a sharp pity for her.

'If I were you,' she said, 'I'd stay right where you are—you'll like it better. And you won't be lonely.'

'I'd rather be lonely than be with Miss Armstrong!'

Paul cut in abruptly, 'Perhaps Miss Armstrong would rather be lonely than be with you. Thought of that?'

The child regarded him with astonishment and indignation, decided to ignore him, then turned to Helen.

'I'd rather be with you. May I share your cabin?'

'I'm afraid not. Ship's personnel—that's a grand word for the people who work on the ship—have special quarters. But you can visit me, if Miss Armstrong doesn't mind. In fact, if she can spare you right now, you can come and watch me unpack.'

'Some people have all the luck,' muttered Paul at her side.

Helen checked a smile and continued, 'May she come, Miss Armstrong?'

The cowed Miss Armstrong threw her a glance of undying gratitude, murmuredl something about unpacking also, and fled.

Outside Helen's cabin Paul said, over the child's head, 'So you are going to spoil her, too. Personally, I'd give her a good walloping.'

'I don't think that would help much,' Helen answered quietly.

The child threw them a dark, suspicious

glance.

'What are you whispering for? I'll bet you're talking about *me* . . .'

'Don't flatter yourself,' Paul snapped, and went on his way.

*　　　*　　　*

Carol perched upon Helen's bed, chattering happily. All signs of temper had evaporated. 'She'd be a quite normal little girl if she'd had a normal upbringing,' thought Helen. Even now, there was hope for her. The bright smile, the eager desire for friendship, the frank enjoyment of buns and milk eaten picnic-fashion whilst Helen unpacked, showed that. In between mouthfuls she chattered about the film they were going to Buenos Aires to make. 'Mummy wouldn't go without me. She won me, you know . . .'

Like a prize in a raffle or an object in a sale, Helen thought in distress.

'Tell me about the film—' she suggested.

'I don't know much about it, 'cept that it's the best part Mummy's ever had. That's why she's in love with Mr. Hennell, I think, because he wrote the book.'

Startled at such adult perception, Helen could say absolutely nothing.

'She wants me to call him Uncle Keith— that's his name, you know. Keith Hennell. But I won't, 'cos he's not my uncle and I'm tired of

26

every boy-friend of Mummy's wanting me to call him that. But he's nice. Nicest of all, so far.' A bleak little note touched the child's voice. 'Not as nice as Daddy, of course . . .'

There was a brief knock upon the door and a voice called, 'May I come in?' And there was Lola Montgomery herself—tall and beautiful and spectacular, with Paul standing behind her.

'Miss Armstrong told me you'd taken the child over, so I called at the surgery and Doctor Brent brought me along.' Her expressive eyes lingered appreciatively on Paul. '*So* kind of him. And kind of you, too, Sister. And now that silly woman is lying on her bed declaring she feels sea-sick already, so *I* must see to Carol!' She held out a long, bejewelled hand to her daughter . . . blood-red fingernails and rows of jangling bracelets. But beneath her theatrical and very striking exterior there was something Helen liked, all the same. If she hadn't been born with so much beauty, so much sex appeal, so much talent, perhaps she would have been a nice, ordinary woman . . .

'Come along, poppet—time for tea!'

'I've had it. Sister ordered it. And I drank a whole pint of milk!'

Her mother was surprised. Milk, said that tiresome Miss Armstrong, was one of the things the child just wouldn't swallow. And yet this nurse had succeeded.

27

Lola studied Helen reflectively. A nice girl. Sensible and modern. The kind she should have employed to take care of Carol, but the bureau hadn't sent along anyone like her. Just a lot of pathetic old women who were absolutely useless, or inefficient young girls eager for a free trip abroad. 'Can't you look after her yourself?' Keith had said, making her feel that somehow she was shirking her duty—but Keith, as yet, hadn't an idea what it was like to be a film star. One was on show all the time, so how could one play at being mother, in between?

But if Carol had taken a liking to this nurse, which she obviously had, and if the nurse was able to control her, which she obviously was, and if the Armstrong woman was likely to prove a dead loss, which was equally obvious, it would be wise to cultivate Sister Cooper . . .

Lola smiled her ravishing smile, the one which had flashed from so many screens and sent hearts spinning from the stalls to the back of the balcony, and said, 'I insist that you come to my party to-night—you *and* the doctor. Cocktails at six, in my state-room. And I won't *hear* of a refusal!'

CHAPTER FOUR

Lola's state-room was packed from portholes to door. 'The best thing to do on these occasions is to ram your way through,' Paul said in Helen's ear, 'but take care of that nice dress—it's almost as pretty as you are. You look ravishing this evening, by the way.'

Helen laughed, caught up in excitement. The room was crammed with people—gold braid and uniforms mingling with bearded types in sandals and girls in skin tight sweaters. She was introduced to Mike Saunders, the director, and Murray Peterson, who was to play opposite Lola—handsome, but dull, Helen thought at once. And Belita Cortez was there, looking enchanting. 'My dear, I couldn't overlook a millionaire's daughter, could I?' Lola said in an aside.

Lola had seized upon Helen at once. 'That child of mine absolutely refuses to go to bed— if there's a party going, she *must* be in on it. Besides, she knew you were coming. She's taken a great liking to you, Sister, which is a relief to me, I must confess, for that stupid woman I employed to look after her is a dead loss—an absolute *dead loss.* Keith says I should have insisted upon a fully-trained nurse, but what does a bachelor know about such things? I thought a kindly, motherly soul would be the answer, but the Armstrong is past it, my dear, absolutely past it . . .'

Helen experienced a swift pity for poor Miss Armstrong, who was propping up the wall, looking pea-green, whilst Carol darted in and out of the guests, gladly evading her.

'I'll take over,' Helen said impulsively. 'You go to bed, Miss Armstrong. I'll bring Carol along later and tuck her up for the night.'

When Miss Armstrong had tottered gratefully out into the corridor, Lola said fervently, 'Bless you, Sister! You were obviously sent from heaven. But you haven't a drink! Doctor—grab drinks for yourself and Sister, will you? Look, I just can't go on calling you Sister—it's so horribly antiseptic! What's your Christian name? Helen? Then I'll call you Helen. I do wish Keith would come—he's the author of this wonderful book we're filming, and I'm relying on him to play host for me to-night.' Something in her tone implied that it was his natural right to do so.

So that's the way it is, thought Helen. She's in love with him. And he with her? Obviously, since she spoke of him so possessively.

'You haven't met him, have you, Helen? My dear, he's the most interesting man I've met in years—but why he had to set that wonderful novel against a drab industrial background, I just don't know, and so I told him. It was Mike's idea to switch to a more glamorous setting. Keith protested, but was overruled, of course. Authors always are! "Just you wait until you're established," I told him, "and then you can fling your weight around." And he's going to be established pretty soon, if I have anything to do with it. Everyone—even the critics—say he's a man of the future.'

'I'd like to meet him,' Helen said politely. 'I thought the book quite brilliant.'

'Of course! *He* is brilliant! We're going a long way together, he and I.' She gave a tinkling laugh. 'But like all brilliant people, he seems to have no idea of time. I *wish* he would come!'

And at that precise moment the door opened. Helen saw it open, because she was watching Paul's progress through the crowd, precariously balancing drinks, and across his shoulder she saw the man who entered.

'Here he is, at last!' Lola cried, and pushed everyone aside as she hurried to meet him. And then, flinging her arms about his neck, she kissed him full upon the mouth.

Someone put a glass in Helen's hand—she didn't even know that it was Paul. She didn't even hear his voice as he said, 'There you are, darling—won with blood, toil, tears and sweat, so drink up and enjoy it!' His voice ceased abruptly. 'What's the matter?' he asked lightly. 'Seen a ghost?'

A ghost, thought Helen. Yes—a ghost from the past. The ghost of David Henderson, looking at her across the crowded room. Just a little older, just a little greyer, just a little sterner.

David Keith Henderson——Keith Hennell, the author. The man who had written so stirringly about a doctor's struggles, a doctor's life. And she hadn't even suspected. Why should she? And there he was, walking back into her life as abruptly as he had walked out of it.

CHAPTER FIVE

It wasn't true, of course. She was imagining it, dreaming it. But those were David's eyes looking at her with undisguised astonishment and recognition.

Their glance was brief, but intense and startling. A moment later he was caught in the crowd, carried forward on Lola's possessive arm, and Helen heard Paul's voice saying, 'Drink up, darling. This promises to be quite a party, so let's get into the spirit of the thing.'

Slowly she came back to the present, back from that dim horizon of shock and disbelief. She was aware that her heart was pounding and that she was trembling, although she was glad to observe that her hand was steady as she took the glass Paul held out.

'Well,' he said cheerfully, 'here's to us!'

She raised her glass mechanically and drank

with him. She even made conversation, not only with Paul, but with those around her, but all the time she was aware of David Henderson towering head and shoulders above the majority of the guests, and that every now and then his head would turn and look in her direction.

Slowly, he edged his way towards her, with Lola's possessive hand clutching his arm. He was deliberately seeking her out, even though such a short time ago—was it really three years—he had turned upon his heel and left her.

A little flame of anger darted through Helen's mind. Did he think he could drop her, just like that, and then greet her again as if nothing had happened between them, as if the months they had worked together had been meaningless and the outings they had shared, the pleasures they had enjoyed, the companionship they had known, mattered no more than the fleeting passing of time?

The room was becoming more crowded at every moment. People were jostling against each other, many of whom, Helen suspected, were gate-crashers. Paul had become separated from her. He was sandwiched between Lola's leading man, Murray Peterson, and Mike Saunders, the film director, and in a distant isolated corner Belita Cortez was looking shy and a little overwhelmed.

David's dark head drew nearer. Helen

waited for him. Her first shock had receded, but it was no use pretending to herself that she wasn't stirred by the encounter or that the intensity of her reaction wasn't startling. She felt more than surprise, more than shock, and suddenly she was asking herself why she should be so disturbed by a man whose memory she had firmly rejected.

At last, he was beside her, Lola's hand still clutching his arm. Helen saw the film star's fingers, long and tapering, with blood-red talons holding his sleeve in a claw-like grasp.

He looked down from his great height and said: 'Hallo, Helen.'

That was all. It seemed trite and conventional and inadequate, and so did her answer: 'Hallo, David.'

'Do you two know each other?' Lola inquired brightly. There was an undertone of pique in her voice.

'We've met,' Helen told her.

David said, 'Long ago.'

He held out his hand to Helen, dislodging Lola's fingers. He stepped aside to let someone pass and the movement brought him close to Helen's side. Lola was soon engulfed by an admiring, chattering group, leaving David and Helen together.

'This is a surprise,' he said, thinking what a dull, conventional opening it was. But what else could he say? That he was stunned, overjoyed? He was both, so much so that in

34

the brief moment when he had looked across the room and recognised her, his heart seemed to stand still.

Indeed, life itself had stood still, carrying him back three years—back to the most important and disturbing time of his life.

'You look well, David.'

'You, too, Helen.'

She laughed lightly.

'What trite conversation one makes at parties!'

'Even when meeting someone after a lapse of time,' he agreed.

She was looking extremely pretty in a simple, but very elegant, little cocktail dress. He had seen her out of uniform before, when they had dined and danced together, and gone to theatres or exhibitions or art galleries, but always he had remembered her in her uniform, with her young face framed by the immaculate starched cap and her hair curling attractively about it. This was the picture David had carried in his mind and, he realised now, in his heart.

'It's a surprise to find you travelling aboard this ship,' he said, again wondering why he failed to find the right words for such a momentous meeting.

'I'm not a passenger. I'm ship's nurse.'

He was even more surprised.

'So you've left St. Christopher's?'

She told him when, and how, and why. 'I've

35

always wanted to travel,' she finished lightly, 'and this seemed a good opportunity.'

'I'm sorry about your mother,' he told her. 'I think you were right to take a job like this. But St. Christopher's will miss you.'

She was tempted to say that the hospital had missed him, too, but instinct warned her not to refer to the past.

'How did you come to get this job?' he asked, chiefly to make conversation. It seemed ridiculous that it should be so difficult to talk to someone with whom he had once been so close, but them was an inevitable restraint between them, and who was to blame for that? he thought ruefully. Himself, of course. He had erected a barrier which could not be overcome in five minutes.

But did he really want to overcome it? He had made a fresh life for himself, rejecting the old one completely, and that meant rejecting everyone and everything in it.

'Dr. Brent recommended me,' Helen told him. 'He's the one I have to thank.'

Her glance travelled in Paul's direction and David, recognising the uniform of a ship's doctor, said:

'Is that he, talking to the pretty girl in the corner?' Helen was glad to see that little Belita Cortez was no longer alone. She was talking animatedly to Paul, her face alight, her eyes sparkling, obviously enjoying herself. Paul was looking down at her with his friendly smile.

They were separated from herself and David by at least a dozen people so, unless Lola returned to claim her man of the moment, they could be alone together for a few moments longer.

Helen was disturbed to find how passionately she desired just that. Sometimes, in the dividing years, she had resolved that if she ever met David Henderson again, she would be cold, frigid, aloof. Instead, she was disturbed to the depths of her being.

'Surely,' he said, 'a job at St. Christopher's held better prospects than that of ship's nurse?'

'Perhaps. But why should I worry about prospects? I'm young. Why should I be doomed to spend all my life in the same hospital corridors?' Her chin lifted. She looked him straight in the eye and finished, 'After all, you made a fresh start with your life, so why shouldn't I do the same?'

'Why, indeed?' he answered, wondering why he found it impossible to get near her again. He wasn't the only one, it seemed, who had erected a barrier.

Her manner was polite, but nothing more, as she said conversationally, 'And what have you been doing all this time?'

'Writing hard.'

'With success, apparently. Congratulations on your book, by the way. I read it and enjoyed every word. Of course, I didn't realise that you were Keith Hennell. Why didn't you write it under your own name?'

'Because I've put David Henderson behind me, once and for all.'

His tone was chilling, intimating that he lived in the present and that no reference to the past would be welcomed. Very well, she thought angrily, if you want to put me firmly in my place, I won't step out of it!

'Good luck with the film,' she said with frigid politeness. 'I hope it will be as successful as the book, David.'

'Thank you, Helen.'

Lola's voice cut in, 'Why do you call him David? His name is Keith.'

Helen saw the film star's coldly beautiful face regarding her with curiosity faintly tinged with suspicion. She was spared the difficulty of answering, however, by David himself.

'They are both my Christian names. Helen knew me by my first one. My real name is David Keith Henderson. Your glass is empty, Lola. Let me get it refilled for you.'

He was gone, shouldering his way through the crowd with Lola at his side.

Helen felt suddenly bereft and alone, shaken more than she cared to admit. She turned away blindly, seeking the reassurance of Paul's company, needing his affection and loyalty. He would never rebuff her as David Henderson had done.

She edged her way to the far corner, where

38

Paul and the enchanting little Belita were now laughing together in mutual enjoyment. They didn't even see her as she approached, but when she spoke his name Paul turned quickly.

'So here you are, darling! I was wondering where you'd got to.'

It didn't really seem like it, she thought with an inner smile. In fact, a looker-on would have believed that he had eyes for no one but the pretty little South American. And no one would have blamed him.

Belita's dark eyes regarded Helen shyly. Paul introduced them.

'Belita was just giving me an imitation of her late school mistress,' he said. 'She's quite a little actress. We'll have to get this film director to give her a test.'

Belita gave a shocked little laugh. 'My father would never hear of such a thing!'

'I don't blame him,' Helen said frankly. 'You're much too nice for that sort of life.'

'Thank you.'

Belita smiled shyly. This girl with the smooth fair hair and the clear English complexion didn't look a bit like her idea of a nurse. Weren't they normally all starch and antiseptic?

The endearment with which Paul greeted Helen did not escape the girl's notice. It even stirred a swift and unaccountable little pang of envy. Was this handsome ship's doctor a little in love with his nurse? The thought touched

Belita's young heart with a sense of disappointment, but she thrust it down with the reflection that if they were in love, these two, it couldn't really be surprising. They made a very handsome couple. Why shouldn't they be well matched in every way?

CHAPTER SIX

Helen was soon caught up in the whirl of shipboard life and the interest of her job. Life was neither dull nor quiet, for the ship's surgery was a very busy place. Paul's prediction about the passengers proved to be correct and after only twenty-four hours at sea the more queasy amongst them began to be troubled with the inevitable seasickness. But these were trivial complaints which could be attended by the stewardesses.

There was always plenty to do in the surgery, which carried an impressive and up-to-date supply of drugs and medicines. The medical staff consisted of herself, Paul, and an orderly to attend to routine chores and to help in sick bay when necessary.

There were three wards, for men, women and children, and an isolation ward for infectious cases. This trip, however, carried no seriously ill passengers, so apart from routine work during the day there were no long stretches of night duty to be faced. This left Helen free to enjoy the social life of the ship each night.

She made a good many friends and began to enjoy the popularity which Paul chaffingly told her he resented.

'I brought you on this ship to be with me, not to be pursued by every man aboard!'

She laughed and told him not to be ridiculous, checking the impulse to add that one man, at any rate, didn't seek her out. And that was David.

Since their first meeting she had scarcely seen him. They had passed each other on deck or in the dining room; they had met in the ship's bar and shared after dinner coffee wich a group of passengers in the lounge. But never again had they been alone.

Helen had the uncomfortable conviction that David avoided anything more than a conventional greeting. Well, she thought, if that's the way he wants it, that is the way *I* want it, too!

She did her best to dismiss him from her mind, but it wasn't easy. Nor was it easy to overlook his close companionship with Lola Montgomery. They were inseparable, these two, sharing the same table in the dining-room and adjoining chairs on the promenade deck. Their close companionship, Helen felt, had a disturbing significance.

She was not alone in her opinion. The

association between film star and author soon became the target for speculation. Not that Helen had much time to spare for shipboard gossip. Paul had warned her that it was the chief occupation of passengers at sea, for a ship was a confined, close-knit little community, cut off from the world—a self-contained little colony in which relationships became emphasised and emotions personal and intense. People became important to each other and then, when the ship docked, were quickly forgotten.

But Lola would not be forgotten by David, for they would still be working together, seeing each other daily. So what was to prevent their relationship from becoming even more important, more personal? Not that it mattered to herself, Helen mused as she worked in the surgery one morning. When the *Carrioca* reached Buenos Aires they would go out of her life for ever, and if, by some misfortune, the film unit made the return voyage on the same ship she would see the passenger list in advance and take good care to avoid any encounter with him.

But that was leaping ahead to the future, and the future was something Helen didn't want to think about. It was better to live in the moment, to seize every job that would keep her mind occupied and never to wonder just why it was necessary to evade all thought of a future which held the promise of happiness—

happiness as Paul's wife.

Just why didn't she want to think about it? She was terribly fond of Paul, and day by day her affection for him increased, as he had said it would. There was satisfaction in working with him, too, for he was a conscientious doctor, keen on his job. But when he began planning for the future, when he said, 'After we're married, Helen, I'll give up this roving life and settle down in a steady G.P.'s practice,' her heart shied away, so that she was filled with a sense of shame and fear.

Was it merely marriage she was afraid of— or marriage with Paul?

She thrust the question aside, resolutely. She had admitted, when she became engaged to him, that her love was not deep and passionate, but she had believed it to be sufficient for marriage.

And so it would be, she resolved suddenly. It would be more than sufficient. It would grow deeper and strong every day, for Paul's character was endearing: he was kind, amusing and gay. Life with him would be serene and happy, undisturbed by violent passion or deep emotion. Many of the happiest marriages in the world were based upon such a footing, so why shouldn't hers be?

Wilkins the medical orderly, a cheerful cockney who had spent most of his life at sea, was chattering with his usual animation as he polished and scrubbed. At the dispensary counter, Helen scarcely heeded him. Wilkins's conversation was a genial flow to which she had quickly grown accustomed. One had only to make punctuating noises and he was quite happy. She could do her own work and think her own thoughts to the accompaniment of his chatter, so it was a few minutes before Helen realised that something he had said was of personal interest to her.

She looked up and asked, 'What was that you said, Wilkins?'

He was in the adjoining room with the door open between them. Now he raised his voice and called, 'I was talking about that there film star, Sister. Seems fair struck on that author-bloke. What's the betting he's lined up to be 'er next 'usband?'

Helen tested the seals of some gelatine capsules she was preparing and answered carefully, 'Shipboard gossip, Wilkins. I'm surprised you listen to it.'

In her own ears the words sounded a little prim, but in her heart she knew they were defensive. Suddenly, she was angry with herself. Why should she care if gossip linked David's name with Lolas?

Wilkins called back cheerily, 'Scandal relieves the monotony of life at sea, Sister. After a couple of voyages you'll be enjoying it as much as the rest of us.'

'There are lots of couples on board this ship who appear to be inseparables,' Helen pointed

44

out, 'but they are allowed to go their own sweet way without speculations as to whether they are going to be married or not.'

'Ah, but they're not people in the public eye. Lola Montgomery is the chief attraction on this ship. And that ain't surprising!'

'No, I suppose it isn't. She's very beautiful.'

Helen stacked the capsules neatly into boxes and set them aside, then she took the drug book from her desk and began to go through it. It was an unnecessary job because drugs had been checked before sailing, but she told herself it was as well to keep up to date with her stocks, refusing to acknowledge that she wanted to occupy her mind in order to reject Wilkin's disturbing observations.

'If you ask me,' Wilkins continued, 'the one I feel sorry for is that kid of hers.'

'Little Carol? Why?'

' 'Cos nobody likes 'er and I can't say I blame 'em. She's a handful, all right, but I'm thinking it's not her fault. If my kids at 'ome be'aved the way she does, my missus would go for 'em good and proper! But what does that kid's mother do? Takes no notice, or tells her to run away—or laughs, if she feels in the mood. And that old geyser she's got to look after 'er, ain't much good.'

'Miss Armstrong is a bad sailor,' Helen said tactfully.

'That she is! 'Alf the time she's prostrate up on deck, with the kid running wild.'

This, Helen knew, was true. For the last three evenings she herself had put Carol to bed, out of pity for Miss Armstrong. It never seemed to enter Lola's head to execute any duties for which she had engaged someone else.

'I will say this,' Wilkins continued chattily, 'that author, Keith Hennell, handles the child better than either of those women.'

It was at that moment that the door opened and Lola herself appeared. She was wearing a spectacular costume of black velvet toreador Pants with a skin-tight sweater, more suitable for cabaret than shipboard wear, Helen thought. But she looked magnificent in it, every curve of her shapely body well defined.

She gave Helen a warm and friendly smile. 'Ah, there you are, Sister!'

Why does she make it sound as if she didn't expect to find me here? Helen wondered. Obviously she came to the ship's surgery for a purpose, and as Paul is off duty that purpose must be to see me.

'What can I do for you, Miss Montgomery?'

Lola made a little *moue* of distaste.

'Darling, not Miss Montgomery, please! Everyone calls me Lola. Why can't you?'

Because I don't want to, thought Helen. But aloud she answered, 'Just as you wish.'

'It makes it all so much more personal and friendly, don't you think? And since my own child calls you Helen, I refuse to stand on formality.'

'Where is Carol?' Helen asked, glad to change the subject.

Lola rolled her expressive eyes heavenwards and made gesture of despair.

'Running wild, my dear—absolutely wild! But what can I do about it? That wretched Armstrong woman is now prone upon her bunk.'

'She's a bad sailor,' Helen said for the second time. 'That is something over which no one has any control.'

'Then she should have warned me when I engaged her,' Lola answered petulantly. 'I asked if she was a good sailor and she assured me that she was. Now I discover that the nearest she's ever been to a ship was a pleasure steamer on the Thames!'

'I'll give you some capsules for her. One of these every four hours ought to help.'

Lola took the pills unwillingly. 'I'm not her nurse,' she pointed out, 'but if they'll help to put the silly creature on her feet again I'll give them to her.'

She flashed her vivid smile again, making it even more friendly and appealing.

'That child of mine has taken quite a fancy to you, Helen.'

'I'm very fond of Carol,' Helen answered, guessing what was coming. Lola wanted her to look after the the child. Her overture was not one of friendliness, but of strategy. She was a woman who went through life making use of people.

'So while Miss Armstrong is ill,' Helen said evenly, 'you would like me to keep an eye on Carol, is that it?'

'Darling, how sweet of you to offer! I wouldn't dream of imposing, but after all, you *are* the ship's nurse . . .'

That doesn't make me official children's nurse, Helen thought inwardly, but let it pass.

'I'll be glad to look after Carol. I like her.'

Lola gushed, 'That's absolutely charming of you, Helen dear, and I do appreciate it, especially in view of the fact that she's an outrageous little handful and well I know it! Of course, I absolutely *adore* her, and I'd look after her myself if only my job gave me time, but a film star simply can't call her life her own!'

'I didn't know you were filming during the voyage.'

'We're not actually shooting,' Lola answered smoothly, 'but, of course, there are endless conferences and rehearsals and I have absolutely *reams* of lines to learn. So you do see, don't you, that with that tiresome Miss Armstrong laid low, Carol must be looked after by *some*one?'

'Send her along to me whenever you like,' Helen suggested unwisely. She knew what she was letting herself in for. As Lola said, Carol was a handful, but Helen believed she

48

could be controlled if handled the right way.

'David Henderson is very good with her,' Helen commented negligently.

Lola's face lit up. 'Oh, David is *wonderful* with her, and Carol is absolutely devoted to him, which is terribly lucky.'

'Is it?'

'Well, of course, darling! Not all the men in my life take very favourably to that child of mine.'

Blowing Helen a theatrical kiss, Lola made a very effective exit.

Helen closed the drug book with a little slam.

'If anyone wants me,' she called to Wilkins, 'I'll be up on deck. I need a good breath of fresh air.'

'Right, Sister,' Wilkins answered cheerfully. 'And while you're gorn I'll open all these port 'oles and let that stinkin' perfume out. My, but she's a smasher, though, ain't she?'

I'd like to smash *her!* Helen thought savagely, as she left the surgery.

She could see Lola's magnificent figure walking away down the long corridor, swinging her hips in the provocative fashion for which she was famous. It wasn't a natural walk, it was studied and flamboyant, a deliberate posture which Helen found distasteful. But I suppose David likes it, she thought furiously. I suppose even as intelligent a man as he can be besotted!

49

CHAPTER SEVEN

Lola went on her way to Miss Armstrong's cabin and, opening the door, saw the unfortunate woman lying weakly against her pillows. She looked pathetic and ill and, for a moment, even Lola's selfish heart was touched with a fleeting pity.

'I've brought some pills. Sister Cooper says you're to take one every four hours. I'll give you one now.'

She went into the bathroom and returned with a glass of water.

Miss Armstrong took the tablet gratefully. 'I'm being an awful nuisance,' she murmured abjectly.

'You certainly are, but I suppose you can't help it. All I hope is that you get well quickly, for all our sakes. Sister Cooper has promised to keep an eye on Carol, but that mustn't encourage you to take a long time over getting better.'

Lola put a note of censure into her voice, just to emphasise their relationship. The right way to handle underlings, she believed, was to keep them firmly in their place.

Miss Armstrong said meekly, 'That's terribly kind of Sister Cooper.'

'I'm glad you appreciate it.'

'I do hope Dr. Brent won't mind.'

'I don't see why he should.'

'If she gives up her spare time to Carol he might.'

'Why?' Lola asked with idle curiosity.

'Because they're always together.'

Lola's eyes revealed a spark of interest.

'Is that so? Then, despite being sick, you've noticed more than I have.'

For the first time she smiled at the unfortunate woman. For the first time she even experienced a kindling of liking, as one felt towards the bearer of good news. If this were true, if there was actually something between the ship's doctor and Sister Cooper, there was no need to feel suspicious about Helen's acquaintance with David.

Ever since that meeting in her state-room Lola had been curious about it. It was true that since that day she had never seen them alone together, and she had taken very good care to keep David at her side, but the suspicion that they had known each other well had persisted quite illogically. Once she had even tried to question David. 'How long have you known Sister Cooper?' she had asked. 'And how well?'

'A long time, and very well,' David answered calmly—which told her precisely nothing.

Lola said casually, 'Do you mean they are in love, those two?'

Miss Armstrong checked a moan. It was an effort to make conversation, but this woman was her employer and even at death's door would expect her undivided attention. But if only she would go away! If only the ship would sink to the bottom of the ocean and stay there?

'I don't know, Miss Montgomery, I'm sure. I just see them together a lot . . .'

'On *and* off duty?'

'Yes.'

'And you think Doctor Brent would mind if someone else, even little Carol, took her from him?'

'I said—I hoped he wouldn't—'

'But, nevertheless, you believe he would. That means he is rather more than interested in her, don't you think?'

That was just what Miss Armstrong did think. She had thought so, many times, as she sat in her sheltered corner of the deck, hoping to die. At first she had watched Sister Cooper because hers was the only friendly face in an alien world, and through bleak, unhappy eyes she had observed the nurse's trim figure stepping briskly about her duties. She had watched for her as if for a ministering angel, and gradually become aware that someone else watched for her, too—the ship's doctor. That had awakened the first flicker of interest in Miss Armstrong's unhappy heart. If there was anything she loved it was a nice romance, and if only she had been well enough to enjoy it, here was one, right under her nose, with all the ingredients she liked—a

52

handsome hero, an attractive heroine, a shipboard background. Uniforms, glamour, the lot.

'Well, *don't* you?' Lola persisted mercilessly.

'Oh, yes—yes, indeed,' the woman murmured wretchedly. 'I think they make a wonderful couple so—so handsome and romantic . . .'

She subsided with a little groan, and Lola laughed. 'My dear Miss Armstrong, what a sentimentalist you must be, to think of romance even when you're sea-sick! I suppose you really *are* ill, and not just faking it to get out of coping with Carol?' When Miss Armstrong uttered a protesting moan, Lola added with a genuine twinge of compassion, 'No, I can see you're not. You're positively pea-green! Never mind—just keep on taking those pills, and in the meantime, if this medical romance flourishes, I'll keep you posted! And now I'll leave you to your misery.'

When she had gone, Miss Armstrong turned her face into her pillow and wept. Were all beautiful women cruel? she thought unhappily. Did they all enjoy tormenting those less fortunate? And to think that the prospect of this job had seemed glamorous and exciting, promising to transform her into a world of which, hitherto, she had only dreamed! But she had never dreamed that it would be like this, prostrating her with sickness and tormenting her with a child of whom she was

53

absolutely terrified. Nor had she dreamed that the lovely Lola, whom she had admired from the two-and-nines for years, would prove to be so hard, so merciless, so completely opposed to the enchanting creature of her films.

The ship give a gentle roll. To Agatha Armstrong it seemed to lurch up one side of the globe and slide down the other. She clutched the handrail of her berth and groaned. She could let herself go now, because there was no one within earshot.

But she was wrong. A voice beside her said unexpectedly, 'I'm sorry you're ill, really I am. Can I do anything for you?'

The woman lifted heavy lids and saw Carol regarding her with surprising concern. For once, the child's defiant petulance was absent.

Miss Armstrong shook her head mutely.

'I'll be all right, dear. Sister Cooper sent me some pills.'

'Oh, well, in that case you're sure to get well.'

I wish the child had as much confidence in *me,* thought the unfortunate woman.

Unexpectedly, Carol placed a soft little hand on her fevered brow.

'Does that help? It should. It's what nurses do. And they feel a patient's pulse, like this, and take their temperature by sticking a glass tube in their mouths. I'm going to be a nurse when I grow up, like Sister Cooper.'

Agatha felt too ill to reply. She wished the

child would go away. But Carol had no such intention, and suddenly advanced with a toothbrush, wanting to play at nurses by sticking the handle beneath the patient's tongue in place of a thermometer. Miss Armstrong recoiled. 'No, dear, no! Go away! Go and find Sister Cooper—she has promised to look after you . . .'

Carol's face lit up.

'Goody!' she cried, dropping the toothbrush and racing to the door. It slammed heavily behind her . . .

Agatha Armstrong winced, and wished again that she could die.

CHAPTER EIGHT

Helen was glad to see Paul on deck. He was reclining lazily upon a deck chair, enjoying the sun. He held out his hand to her and said, 'Come and join me. Take Belita's chair—she won't mind.'

'Where is she?'

'Playing quoits with Lola Montgomery's author. He's off the leash while Lola has her hair done.'

'You make him sound like a lap-dog,' Helen said, sinking into the adjoining deck chair.

'Well, isn't he?'

'Certainly not.'

Paul regarded her with one quizzical eyebrow raised.

'You're hot in his defence, my love. How come?'

'I'd be hot in the defence of anyone unjustly criticised or condemned.'

'I'm not condemning him. I like the fellow. Not that I've talked to him much—he's the reserved type. Except with Lola.'

That was true enough, Helen thought wretchedly, and very much against her will and better judgment she asked impulsively, 'Is he in love with her, *really* in love with her, do you think?'

'I wouldn't know, but it looks like it. And yet . . .'

Paul broke ofd, frowning thoughtfully in the direction of the sports deck, where David's tall, athletic figure was engaged in a vigorous game with the agile little Belita.

'And yet what?'

'And yet I shouldn't think a chap like that would let anyone know what he was thinking, or feeling. As I said, he's reserved. And, as *you* said, he's not a lap-dog. So he wouldn't be feeding out of Lola's hand unless he enjoyed it, I imagine.'

'I haven't noticed him eating out of her hand.'

'But they're always together. Of course, that might well be Lola's doing. A demanding woman, the Montgomery. Not like you, my sweet. You're so undemanding as to be almost elusive. I never have you to myself these days, except in the surgery, and then Wilkins is always hanging around, damn him. How can I make love to my nurse before his watchful eyes?'

In the shadow between their deck chairs, Paul's hand found hers, and squeezed it. She returned the gesture, gratefully and impulsively. 'I'd have you know I'm on duty, Doctor!' she pointed out demurely. 'You should reprimand me for evading my work.'

A burst of laughter echoed from the sports deck. Belita's light and gay, David's deep and strong. He was a man who laughed rarely and the sound of it was a nostalgic echo in Helen's mind. Long ago, they had laughed together, in much the same way.

An unaccountable pain touched her heart and she turned away so that Paul should not observe any betrayal.

It was at that moment that little Carol raced up a nearby companionway and hurled herself into Helen's lap. 'I've been looking *everywhere* for you' she cried. 'Is it true you're going to look after me for the rest of the voyage?'

'It certainly is not! Only until Miss Armstrong is better. And well you know it, you minx.'

'She's awfully ill. She'll probably stay that way until we reach Buenos Aires. She might even die!'

'What a heartless little hussy you are,' Paul commented bluntly, and Carol looked at him, wide-eyed and hurt. She was still unsure of the doctor; still a little afraid of him. She didn't feel happy and at ease with him, as she did with Keith Hennell, and it was with relief that she saw him coming off the sports deck with Belita. To avoid Paul's discouraging glance she turned, and ran to meet him.

David picked her up, swung her sky high, and perched her upon his shoulder.

'Getting into practice, isn't he?' said Paul.

'Into practice for what?' Helen asked stonily.

'For playing the role of stepfather, of course. Haven't you noticed what a fuss he makes of the kid?'

'I've noticed that he is kind and understanding with her, if that is what you. mean.' Helen rose, saying briskly, 'well, I must get back to work.'

'As your boss, I order you to remain.' Paul's eyes twinkled up at her. 'Come off it, Helen. You know there are no patients queueing up at the surgery door, so what's the hurry? Aren't you enjoying my company?'

His endearing smile melted her heart.

'Just for that,' she said, 'I'll take you on at deck tennis—*and* beat you—the moment the surgery closes for the day.'

'Done!' he cried. 'And then we'll dance until midnight and make love by moonlight.'

'And if there isn't a moon?'

'I'll order one. Specially. A blue moon, at that.'

'I always think a blue moon sounds chilly and unbecoming. I'd rather have the conventional kind—large and glowing.'

'And romantic,' agreed Paul, adding hastily as the others approached, 'I'll order an outsize one, darling, if that's what you want. But I could just as easily make love to you without one.'

David swung Carol down from his shoulders and planted her firmly on the deck. But she clung to his hand, dancing up and down as she chanted excitedly, 'Helen is going to put me to bed! Helen is going to—'

'Sister Cooper, to you,' Paul reprimanded sharply.

The eyes of the older man regarded him levelly, and then his deep voice said to Carol, 'Doctor Brent is quite right. Have you no respect for your elders and betters, my child?' But his tone, and his eyes, were kind.

'Helen said I may call her Helen!' Carol protested. 'Didn't you, Helen?'

'I did, indeed. *"What's in a name?"* she quoted. *"A rose by any other . . ."* '

She turned away, avoiding David's glance, and he stood for a while, watching her go, scarcely aware of Belita's gay chatter and Paul's amiable rejoinders. For a moment Carol regarded the three of them, feeling shut out and unwanted—unwanted even by Uncle Keith. She had started calling him uncle despite her earlier resolve. It was natural and easy to do so, for he was more like an uncle to her than other men whom her mother encouraged her to like. Why should I like them? she thought, rebelliously. *They* don't like *me*. They only pretend to, because they're in love with Mummy, or think they are . . .

Her little mouth drooped suddenly and David, looking down, observed her expression and said quietly, 'What's the matter, old girl? Feeling down in the dumps?'

His unexpected understanding was reassuring and helpful. She nodded bleakly, and he ruffled her hair with an affectionate hand.

'D'you know what I would do, if I were you? I'd ask Helen to tuck you up nice and early to-night, because you've been late to bed since we sailed, and then I'll come down and read a story to you. How's that?'

'Lovely, *lovely*!'

She flung her thin little arms round his knees in a passionate hug of gratitude, then raced towards the surgery. Bursting in unannounced she was surprised to see Sister Cooper staring through a porthole out to sea. Just staring, the way she herself did when she felt particularly lost and alone and bewildered . . .

For a moment Carol waited quietly, then she whispered, 'What's the matter, Helen?'

Helen jerked round.

'Goodness, how you startled me! I didn't hear you come in.'

'I know you didn't. You didn't hear anything. Your thoughts were miles away, weren't they? That's what Daddy used to say when I spoke to him sometimes and he didn't hear, "Sorry, chick," he'd say, "my thoughts were miles away . . ." and then he'd rumple my hair, just the way Uncle Keith does when he feels sorry for me.'

'And why should Uncle Keith, feel sorry for you?' Helen said briskly.

'Because I haven't a father. Or he thinks I haven't.'

What an odd, precocious little child she was, Helen thought pityingly; a mixture of pathos and arrogance, timidity and aggression.

She held out her hand to Carol. 'Come along, poppet—I'll order supper for you in my room, and then read you a story before bedtime.'

'Thank you,' Carol answered gravely. 'I'd like to have supper in your room, but I've promised to let Uncle Keith read a story to me. He likes to, you know it's practice for him.'

'Practice for him?' Helen echoed bleakly.

'For when he's married to Mummy. He'll be a good father to me—she told me so.'

A stupefying sense of shock crept up from Helen's heart, rendering her speechless. She regarded the child's appealing little face, with

61

its worldly-wise, innocent eyes and its wistful mouth, in disbelieving concern. Surely it wasn't true? Surely David wasn't *really* going to marry Lola Montgomery? And yet . . . and yet . . . wasn't he always with her, and wasn't he always attentive to little Carol? Understanding and patient and protective—like a father.

Helen said with forced brightness, 'Time for supper, Carol! Come along . . .'

Later, when she had tucked the child up in bed, speaking in whispers to avoid disturbing the sleeping Miss Armstrong, Carol's thin little arms crept around Helen's neck, detaining her. 'Don't go yet,' she pleaded. 'Not until Uncle Keith comes, at any rate!'

'He'll be along shortly, pet. You can look at this picture book until he arrives.'

'Don't you want to see him?' asked the disconcerting Carol.

'I have work to do.'

'What work?'

'I must tidy the surgery, and then lock it for the night.'

'What if anyone is ill?'

'Then we open up again.'

'It didn't look as if it needed tidying to me, and anyway, there's Wilkins.'

'*Mr.* Wilkins, to you, young lady.'

'Why? Isn't he the same as a steward?'

'You read your picture book . . .'

'Find a story for Uncle Keith to read, then I can tell him you chose it.'

'Anything to delay me!' smiled Helen. 'I know these tactics, you scamp.'

Carol chuckled, and then, with the quick change from gaiety to gravity which was so much a part of her nature, she said bluntly, 'Do you think Uncle Keith will come?'

'Why shouldn't he?'

'Because Mummy will have finished at the hairdresser's ages ago and be all changed for dinner by now, and she'll want him to meet her in the bar.'

Without even troubling to say good night to her child, thought Helen pityingly. She ran a gentle hand through Carol's hair and said, 'I am sure that if Uncle Keith said he would come, he won't break his promise.'

'After he's married to Mummy, he might.'

'What makes you say that?'

'Because he'll be busy writing more parts for her. That's why she really wants to marry him, I think.'

Such adult cynicism in one so young shocked Helen profoundly, and before she could think of an answer the child ran on, 'Of course, I do like him, but only as an uncle. I've got a daddy of my own and don't want any other.'

'Helen gathered the child close and kissed her. 'Good night, poppet. You just read your fairy tales and don't think of anything else.'

What a pathetic, unnatural child Carol was, Helen thought pityingly as she crossed to the door. Despite all her material advantages, she was really a solitary and bereft little thing. But too astute, too adult, too perceptive—and much too vulnerable. Was it true, what she said about her mother and David Henderson? Could David possibly be seeking Carol's affection in order to facilitate their future relationship?

A swift little dart of disgust and anger shot through Helen's heart, so that as she shut the door and turned to find herself face to face with David, she was immediately erect and defensive.

She greeted him formally.

'Good evening, Mr. Hennell.'

His hand was upon the door-knob. He looked at Helen for a long moment, but what his thoughts were she could not even fathom.

'Good evening, Sister. It is good of you to deputise for Miss Armstrong.'

'And you for Carol's father,' Helen retorted crisply.

If he was startled, he didn't show it. His deep-set eyes merely regarded her with deeper intensity, but there was an imperceptive tightening about his mouth as he answered, 'Since Carol is deprived of him, perhaps a deputy is better than nothing, Sister Cooper.'

He shut the door firmly behind him, leaving Helen feeling frustrated and angry and definitely snubbed.

CHAPTER NINE

The ship's dance that night was a gay affair. Most of the passengers had found their sea legs by now and were able to enter into the spirit of the thing. Empty tables in the dining-room were filling up; the lounge was more crowded; there was a general air of relaxation and enjoyment, a determination to make the most of the luxury and leisure of life at sea.

To Belita Cortez this first taste of freedom was like nectar from the gods. Hitherto her life had been bound by school discipline and the even greater authority of a strict Mexican household, for despite their wealth the Cortez family were rigid in their observance of traditional etiquette. No daughter of a well-born South American family was allowed any real taste of freedom until she was ready to be presented, under the strictest chaperonage, into society, and this chaperonage prevailed until her marriage, when she merely exchanged the supervision of her duenna for the jealous control of her husband.

Not without reason had the delicate wrought-iron *rejas* been erected outside the windows of old Mexican houses, exquisite bars to separate lover from beloved. Through her bedroom window at home, Belita could see the South American landscape framed in a

65

delicate tracery of rose and tendril, patterned by the hand of a craftsman who had sympathetically endeavoured to adorn such a restricted view with a form of beauty, however unyielding.

That was why this brief taste of freedom was heaven—almost overpowering in its magic. She knew, of course, that it couldn't last; that when the *Carrioca* finally docked she would say good-bye to emancipation until fortune, or her parents, presented her with a husband. She had no doubt that an early marriage would be arranged for her, and that it would be an advantageous one, but a European education had made her desire a marriage in which the woman was not regarded merely as her husband's chattel, nor set upon an uncomfortable pedestal. Being obedient to one's husband was acceptable only if that state, were voluntary, not commanded. And if I loved, really loved, thought Belita as she brushed her dark shining hair, I would want to please my husband in all things—but only *because* I loved him.

She knew that her father had placed her unser the care of the ship's captain, who had acknowledged his duty by seating her at his table and instructing the purser to see that she had everything she wanted. There his supervision ceased, and very nice, too, thought Belita with a happy smile. There was no one to order her to bed precisely two hours after dinner, no one to say, 'Belita, a young lady of refinement does not patronise the ship's bar nor dance with any young man who requests the pleasure . . .' no one to watch and reprimand and restrict her movements.

And no one to forbid her to join the handsome young ship's doctor for a drink before dinner, which she had promised to do this evening with the greatest of pleasure.

This heady taste of freedom would not last, of course, so she was making hay while the sun shone, and if she could make a great big haystack out of it so much the better. It would be a memory to live on for a very long time. Once home, she would look at her magnificent array of clothes, housed in elaborate wardrobes and carefully looked after by her own personal maid, and remember how she had shed them upon her cabin floor after a night of dancing, dropping into bed in an ecstasy of delightful fatigue, waking again to breakfast in bed and a leisurely selection of the right sporting outfit for the morning's activities. And if those activities included a brief half hour with the ship's doctor, the day was made perfect from the start.

To-night she chose her gown with care, relishing the moment, for when she reached home it would be her mother who would select and command. 'To-night, Belita, your black lace, with your great-grandmother's pearls . . .' or: 'This afternoon, my child, the white shantung . . .' even if one's mood ran to scarlet satin or tight-fitting velvet. She could plead, of course. 'Please, Mamma, not the black lace! The emerald silk. I much prefer the emerald silk!' and, if her daughter had pleased her that day, Señora Cortez would be indulgent, kissing Belita's cheek affectionately and saying, 'As you will, *chiquita*—how can I refuse you anything?' Nevertheless, kind and wonderful as she was, her mother most certainly *could* refuse when her will so desired.

Papa, now, was different. A little coaxing, a little cajolery went a long way to soften his heart. He adored his children, especially his daughters, of whom Belita was the youngest. Even in the question of marriage, she felt, he would not force her against her will—not if she loved another, someone who was upstanding and strong and worthy of her devotion. Someone like Paul Brent, whose job was humane and good and made up for his personal lack of money. A great one for the humanities, was Pedro Cortez, as the world well knew. He had endowed a hospital in Buenos Aires, and another in Mexico City. With his influence could he not make an opening, a good opening, for a son-in-law who was a doctor?

Belita pulled herself up with a jerk, a deep tide of colour flooding her face. She was dreaming impossible dreams; she was allowing desire to run away with common sense. Doctor

Brent was merely being kind to her, that was all. He had taken her under his wing to see that she had a good time—why, he had practically admitted as much! 'Come out of your shell, señorita,' he had commanded gaily, 'and enjoy yourself. If you're too shy, leave it to me. I'll see that you have a good time on this ship, in the right way, with the right people. A girl like you could be the target for a lot of unscrupulous types. I'll keep them at bay. Leave it to Uncle!' And he had smiled in that infectious way of his—kindly, sincerely little knowing that the very sight of that smile made her heart tremble.

It meant nothing, of course. Nothing more than the friendly overtures of a friendly person. He wasn't attracted to her. Why should he be? And how *could* he be, with that charming nurse working at his side all day?

The thought of Sister Cooper quelled Belita's hopes. Compared with the tall, fair English girl what chance had someone fresh from a convent school? Helen Cooper had the poise and assurance of one who was accustomed to standing on her own two feet; she wasn't a shy little miss just emerging into the world. Apart from that, she was thoroughly nice, and Belita liked her. She was probably far more suitable to be Paul's wife, than she.

With one last vigorous sweep of her hairbrush, Belita let her black tresses cascade down her back. Then she propped her chin upon her hands and stared at her reflection in the mirror. 'Grow up,' she told herself sternly. 'Stop being a silly little dreamer. Be sophisticated, nonchalant, blasé! It might even be wise to flirt a little—or could be, if you knew how.' Her mouth drooped disconsolately. The really successful flirts were like Lola Montgomery, who expected all men to fall at her feet and was never disappointed.

But the film star was merely a beautiful, empty shell; a puppet which posed before a camera; a figure which flaunted its curves and its sex appeal—not really a human being at all. 'If Doctor Brent imagined himself in love with Lola Montgomery I'd have no compunction in winning him from her, or trying to,' Belita decided with a worldly-wise air. 'But Helen Cooper—no. She's different. She's nice. She's the type who ought to be his wife—a help-meet who can understand, and share, his work. That is probably why he loves her and why I can never expect him to care for a spoilt, useless little creature like me . . .'

Belita heaved a great sigh, flung open her wardrobe door and stood back reflectively. The white tulle? The scarlet faille? The fuchsia taffeta? Which should it be? Which would *he* like her in? Which, she wondered ruefully, would he even notice her in? At random, she selected the emerald—silk vivid as a jewel, clinging, soft. It had been made by a leading *couturière* and was, she knew, a masterpiece. Her indulgent father had opened an account for her in Paris, for the daughter of so famous a man must always be magnificently dressed.

Dear Papa, she thought tenderly, as she coiled her dark hair in the nape of her neck and added emerald clips to her small, perfectly-shaped ears. Dear Papa, I won't let him down. I will behave myself with the decorum he expects of me. I will not flirt or run wild, no matter what insane impulses drive me. I will remember that I am a Cortez—proud and restrained and oh, so maddeninglyy frustrated!

Studying her reflection in the long mirror before going to meet Paul in the ship's bar, she decided that dear Papa would be well pleased with her appearance. It did him credit—or, more truthfully, it did the Cortez fortune credit. She, like her mother and her sisters, was a walking advertisement for her father's success. But I would rather be the humble wife of a humble doctor, she thought wistfully, as she made her way towards the observation lounge, where the first-class bar was situated.

It was a wide, spacious place in the bows of the ship, with vast curved windows framing a magnificent view of the ocean. It was the meeting-place for pre-dinner cocktails, and as Belita entered a surge of laughter and gaiety greeted her, a little overwhelming at first, but quickly catching her on a surge of excitement.

71

She stood for a moment upon the threshold, a vivid little figure scanning the crowd for a glimpse of Paul. 'Seven o'clock sharp,' he had said. 'And don't be late!'

She wasn't late. She was dead on time. His invitation, she had thought, was personal, significant. It had filled her heart with happiness and hope. But when she saw him her heart sank, for he was not alone. Helen was with him. They were sitting together in a distant corner, surrounded by others—Lola Montgomery, the author Keith Hennell, Lola's leading man Murray Peterson, and Mike Saunders the film director; a gay, chattering crowd.

So Paul's invitation had not been intimate and personal, after all.

Helen saw her first, and beckoned with her customary friendliness. Paul rose and came to meet her, holding out his hand and drawing her into their circle. His touch sent a sudden fire running through her veins.

Conversation was brisk and gay, tossed amongst the group like a bright bubble, but dominated by Lola. She was the star, as always, and to-night she shone very brightly indeed in a dress of silver lamé. Helen was wearing her official evening uniform, a dress of saxe-blue silk with a small cape lined with scarlet and a becoming little nurse's cap. So she was officially on call, Belita observed. When off duty she was allowed to wear civilian clothes, and very attractively she dressed, despite the fact that her entire wardrobe must have cost a hundredth part of Belita's.

The Mexican girl permitted herself the fleeting wish that Sister Cooper might be called away to a patient—preferably more than one during the course of the evening, so that she herself could dance with Paul. But she squashed the hope loyally. Lola Montgomery she would have had no compunction in competing with, but Helen Cooper was too nice, too sincere, too friendly.

'You look very beautiful, Belita,' Helen said. 'That's a lovely gown, and the colour suits you magnificently. Don't you agree, Paul?'

He agreed enthusiastically and Belita gave a shy smile. A warm tide of colour flooded her face, but only David Henderson guessed its true significance. To the others it was merely a flush of pleasure, but—David's shrewd eyes the eyes which still held a physician's discernment—recognised the emotion behind it. Sympathy touched his heart. The girl was so young and so vulnerable that to fall in love with a handsome young man like Doctor Brent was almost inevitable.

His glance crossed to Paul, who was smiling at Belita with friendly liking. It was plain to see that he thought her charming—who didn't?— but that anything deeper than friendliness didn't enter into it as far as he was concerned. Poor little Belita, David thought—and then

73

reflected that she she had the whole of the voyage in which to improve the situation, if she wished. And why not? They would makee a delightful couple, those two.

It was at that precise moment that Paul turned away from Belita to Helen, and immediately the quality of his glance changed significantly. David sat very still, hardly aware that Lola was touching his hand in a possessive fashion, demanding his attention. He sat still because he was startled by something which seemed to emanate between Helen and the ship's doctor—a sense of intimacy which was disturbing.

He felt a quiver of alarm which was quite inexplicable, for he believed he had recovered from his disappointment over Sister Cooper, a disappointment which had lingered with him a long time after leaving St. Christopher's, and all because she had ignored his letter of farewell, the letter which he had written with a sense of inarticulate longing and an overwhelming desire to say more, much more.

If she had replied, even briefly, it would have given him the opening he desired—to write back, asking her to meet him; to see her away from the antiseptic hospital corridors, free from her starched uniform, with all the horror of that court of inquiry behind him. But not the memory of it. That would linger for ever.

But she had ignored his note, refusing even

74

to say that she understood, or wished him luck. He knew that she believed him blameless in that unhappy affair, her loyalty at the investigation had proved that, but he had wanted more than loyalty from her. So much more which, now, could never be expressed or even hoped for.

He had a sudden sense of bleak and terrible loss. He had never been a demonstrative man, although he knew only too well that beneath the mask of reserve with which he concealed his heart he was a passionate man, capable of a deep and ardent love; so passionate that he had always been at pains to hide it from Helen, who was so much younger than himself.

He remembered the moment he had first seen her, walking along the corridor to the children's ward. He had been startled by her youth. He had expected someone older, not a slip of a girl with smooth blonde hair and the face of a madonna. That madonna-like quality had told him why she had so quickly risen to such a position—it testified to her maternal instinct which, the more he worked with her, was the more apparent. She adored children, and they adored her.

And, before long, so did he.

But he was careful not to show it. She should have someone nearer her own age, he thought; some rising young doctor with whom she could be gay and carefree, not a man like himself, who had spent his youth studying medicine and his spare time, since qualifying, in research.

Nevertheless there had been moments when a sense of awareness leapt between them and even he, who had so sternly refused to dream of anything more intimate than friendship, had felt that she responded to the ardour in him; moments of instinctive perception which sparked off a sense of kinship and understanding and passionate awareness. And then he would look down at her smooth young face and tell himself not to be a fool. Dreams were for youth, not for a man of his age and experience.

So he had guarded his secret love, afraid that in revealing it she might reject him altogether. It was better to have the delight of her companionship than loneliness; better to see her, work with her, and to occasionally cherish a few hours with her away from the hospital, than to lose so precious a relationship because he wanted to make it something greater and more permanent. She, he felt, could never want that.

Looking at her now, he decided that he had been right. She was laughing at something Paul Brent had said, her blonde head, crowned with its becoming little cap, thrown back in delight. And the ship's doctor was laughing, too, his eyes enchanted by her, already more than half in love, it seemed.

She had told him the gay young doctor had

76

recommended her had they known each other well—before the voyage? If not, Paul Brent seemed to have made good headway in a very short time.

CHAPTER TEN

Halfway through the evening, when their party had adjourned from the dining-room to the ballroom, Belita her wish. Helen was called to a patient and while she was gone Paul danced with her. Belita moved in a dream, aware, for the first time since emerging from her strict convent life, of a man's nearness and strength, of his arm about her and the hard muscle of his shoulder beneath her hand. He held her lightly and companionably, but to Belita it was her first step into heaven.

After that he danced with Lola, but then he was back, claiming her again. She looked up with a shy smile and he thought how sweet she was. Helen had called her enchanting. 'She's so unselfconscious, so absolutely unaware of her beauty,' she said, and Paul realised now that Helen was right.

So he smiled down at Belita encouragingly. He wanted the kid to enjoy herself. She was a good little dancer and when the music stopped he said, 'You're booked for the next, young lady—don't forget.'

'Unless Sister Cooper comes back,' she retorted with a smile.

She had an enchanting dimple at the corner of her mouth, which charmed him. But her comment about Helen he ignored.

Helen was away long enough for Paul and Belita to have several dances together. They were in the middle of one when she returned.

Lola glanced at the couple significantly and said to Helen, 'Don't they make a delightful pair?'

Yes, thought Helen, Paul and Belita did make a delightful pair—good to look at; carefree; happy; friendly. She felt no twinge of jealousy as she watched them, for she had a sudden desire to dance, to get on to that floor herself. The band was good, urging her feet into its rhythm, and suddenly she heard David say, quietly, 'Will you dance, Helen? It's a long time since we did.'

His arm about her waist seemed to carry her right back into the past.

'Remember the night we danced at the Fifty Club?' Helen asked spontaneously.

'Of course, I remember.'

He might have been referring to a staid night in a parish hall, instead of a few magic hours in which they had been intensely aware of each other, for that had been the first time they had danced together, the first time they had touched one another. All that, of course, he had forgotten. Perhaps it had never meant anything to him. Perhaps the magic of it had existed only in her own heart.

A sense of bleak disappointment touched her, so that she had to force herself to smile when Paul and Belita danced by. Paul waved to her gaily. He was enjoying himself, and Helen was glad. Belita was enjoying herself, too, executing little spins and twirls with uninhibited abandon. She was as brilliant as a peacock in her emerald green gown.

Helen and David danced in silence. To him, she knew, it was merely a duty dance, a politeness, nothing more.

Lola was surrounded by a little court of admirers and he, temporarily, was not needed. When the music stopped he would return to her side, but meanwhile, his arm was about Helen's waist, her hand was in his, and his cheek close to her own. Not touching, but disturbingly near.

When the music ceased they stood for a moment, quite still, then their arms fell away from each other.

'Helen—'

'Yes, David?'

His deep-set eyes regarded her intently, then he said abruptly, 'Nothing,' and they walked back to their table. His hand was beneath her elbow, guiding her, and when she sat down and no longer felt any physical contact with him, she felt suddenly bereft and alone.

Then Paul was in front of her, smiling his cheerful smile, saying to everyone in general, 'This child dances like an angel!' and Belita was looking radiant. But his smile was for Helen, tinged with that special quality—that possessive quality—with which she was becoming increasingly familiar. 'You're mine,' it said 'and don't you forget it.'

When the band struck up again he claimed her immediately. 'We've time to make up,' he told her as he led her on to the floor. 'That patient kept you away too long.'

It was a soft and gentle waltz. He drew her into his arm and laid his cheek against hers. His lips were close to her ear and he whispered, 'I want to make love to you. What d'you say we find a dark corner of the boat deck? Better still, your cabin, or mine.'

'Let's stick to the boat deck.'

'It's safer, I agree. But who wants safety?'

I do, thought Helen. A nice protective fence all about me, shutting out the past, the present, and the future . . .

The thought was a startling one. She wasn't, normally, a girl who retreated from life. Then why did every instinct urge her to retreat now?

There was a silence, then a burst of applause, and in the midst of it, as in a still oasis, she and Paul stood holding each other, waiting for the music to strike up again. Suddenly the lights dimmed, a tango throbbed, and David, sitting in the shadows, watched the revolving couples upon the small dance floor. A spotlight was focused upon them, and into its orbit Paul and Helen floated, dancing smoothly, easily, and intimately.

A voice beside him said wistfully, 'Of course, they are made for each other, aren't they?'

It was Belita's voice, tinged with undisguised envy. But it wasn't that which disturbed David. It was the fact that her comment was true and he knew to whom it referred. Nevertheless, he asked abruptly, 'Who are made for each other?'

'Doctor Brent and Sister Cooper, of course. They're so—so absolutely *right*, don't you agree?'

He didn't agree. He wanted to protest vigorously and vehemently, but could say nothing. The child was imagining it, he told himself. She's jealous, poor mite. She'd feel the same way if he danced with Lola or any other woman present. But in a secret corner of his heart he knew this was untrue. Belita Cortez might be young and inexperienced and falling rapidly in love, but she was without conceit or malice and she had a native courage which enabled her to face facts—this fact; that the man she loved was in love with someone else.

Helen.

The realisation hit him with a sharp impact, but still he denied it. He smiled at Belita indulgently and said, 'Shipboard gossip always links the doctor with his nurse. It means nothing.'

She turned her widely-spaced eyes upon him and said frankly, 'Don't try to comfort me, Mr. Hennell. You're a clever man, I know, you wouldn't be a successful writer otherwise, but don't imagine that by denying facts you can make me deny them, too.'

He was shaken by her wisdom, which he recognised as the unveiled perception of the young. He hoped that life would never hurt or disillusion her; that she would retain her honesty and trust for ever.

He was searching for a tactful answer when Lola's voice cut in:

'But doctors and nurses always fall for each other, don't they? It's in the best romantic tradition. And if rumours are correct these two come from the same hospital . . .'

'Rumours? What rumours?' David said sharply.

Lola looked at him in surprise.

'Just rumours, darling—does it matter?'

'Where did they come from?'

You forget that I have a precocious young daughter. She goes all over the ship, talking to people, and in particular she haunts the ship's surgery. She's got quite a penchant for Sister Cooper—or haven't you noticed? There's also a garrulous medical orderly named Wilkins, always ready for a chat.'

'You don't mean to tell me that Wilkins would gossip with a child?'

'Indeed he would—and does. And you know my Carol—her sole conversation, it seems to me, consists of questions, to which she must always have the answers.'

When he made no reply, Lola gave him a careful sideways glance. This brilliant author was baffling her lately, and nothing annoyed Lola more than to be baffled by someone; to feel out of her depth, or forgotten. 'I was closer to him in London,' she thought resentfully, 'although we had only just met. During those preliminary script discussions there was nothing to distract his attention. But since we sailed something, or some*one* has come between us.'

But what, or who? During the last few days, when she had begun to find David increasingly remote, Lola had felt a mounting suspicion within her—a suspicion which she could not focus upon any particular person. And that annoyed her. It provoked her, too; so much so that she now answered a little tartly

'Carol is an intelligent child—or perhaps you prefer precocious, or spoilt?'

He sensed the sharpness in her voice, and was silent. He wasn't going to reveal his own opinion about Carol, that she was a pitiful, lost little soul badly in need of a mother's love. Was that why she had developed what Lola called a penchant for Helen? If so, it wasn't

83

surprising; he himself remembered how instinctively children had been drawn to Sister Cooper at St. Christopher's. As for himself, his interest in Carol was a protective one. If someone didn't step in and deputise for her father, if someone didn't give her the protection and control she so badly needed, the child would grow up into an outsize problem—bewildered, unhappy, and unloved.

'Would you care to dance, Lola?' he asked politely, half expecting a refusal because he knew how she adored holding court. To sit in a prominent position, surrounded by men, meant more to her than to dance with one man in the middle of a crowded floor, obscured by the rest of the dancers. Unless the spotlight picked her out, of course, and people paused to watch and admire . . .

'I've been waiting for you to ask me,' she said with gentle reproach.

'I'm sorry. I thought you were too greatly in demand to spare the time to dance.'

'I can always spare time for you, darling.'

She wore a sheath dress of some metallic material which glittered subtly as she moved. It was cold beneath his touch, but beneath it he felt the soft curves of her beautiful body. As they danced she pressed it against him briefly. In passing, Helen observed their closeness and said to Paul, abruptly, 'Let's find that corner of the boat deck, Paul.'

He needed no second bidding.

Lola observed their departure and laughed softly.

'What did I tell you? They are slipping away together. Jealous, David?'

'Why should I be?'

'You knew her once upon a time, didn't you?'

'I've already told you that.'

'But not how intimately.'

'Not intimately at all.'

'Then why did you seem to care when I said that they came from the same hospital? You looked quite startled.'

When he made no answer she continued, 'Anyway, it's true, according to that garrulous medical orderly. I was searching for that troublesome child of mine one day, doing the Armstrong woman's job for her while she lay feeling sorry for herself on her bed, and finally tracked Carol down to the ship's surgery. The doctor was on duty, but Sister Cooper was out of the room at the time. Carol was chatting away to Wilkins, who was doing something with a batch of papers, and as I walked in he looked at one in his hand and said, "Where d'you want me to file this, sir?" Doctor Brent asked him what it was and he said it was something to do with Sister Cooper—her appointment form, or something.'

'Well?' asked David carefully.

'Well, Paul told Wilkins to put it on her desk. "It will have to be filed," he said. I called to that little brat of mine and as we went out of the room I heard Wilkins say, " I didn't realise Sister came from the same hospital as you, sir." I was shutting the door then and only heard the doctor say something rather sharp about not reading other people's private documents.' Lola looked up at David with a quizzical glance. 'So it all adds up, doesn't it?'

'To what?'

'Darling, you're very obtuse to-night! To the fact that she came on this trip to be with him! I suppose he wangled the job for her. Mark my words, there's something between those two.'

The music stopped abruptly, and so did David, jerking Lola to a standstill in a way she very much resented. It was a bad exit for her from the dance floor.

It was easy, David found when they returned to their table, to withdraw into silence, for Lola was immediately surrounded by her court and he was forgotten. He didn't have to make conversation with little Belita, for one of the ship's officers came up and claimed her and after that she had a stream of partners. The ship's doctor and nurse did not appear again.

After a while David slipped away quietly. The sports deck, in the stern of the ship, was dark and deserted, offering the refuge he sought. He needed solitude in which to arrange his thoughts, to discipline and control them. Lola's news had stunned him, and in the depths of his reserved heart it hurt, also. He stood at the rail, watching the wake of the ship unfurl like a turbulent white ribbon behind it, slicing the dark stretches of the ocean like an endless road. Life was rather like that, he reflected. An interminable, stormy path which one had to traverse somehow, or go under.

The night air was sharp and he was grateful for it. He lifted his face to the sky and felt the ocean wind beat upon it. So they had known each other before, had they? At St. Christopher's, of all places. That meant their acquaintanceship was not new, as he had imagined, but a thing of long standing. But how long? He didn't remember a Doctor Brent upon the wards, nor even a medical student of that name. How old was he? Young, quite young. He couldn't have been more than a houseman a year or two ago.

A year or two—that meant he might have come to St. Christopher's after he himself had left. *After* that terrible business about the child . . .

Which meant, please God, that he knew nothing about it. That Helen was the only person aboard this ship who knew the story of his past—and she would never betray him.

A sense of relief flooded his mind. But not his heart. There remained an ache which he could not, or would not, explain.

For a long time he stood at the ship's rail, looking out over the darkening ocean, but not seeing it; seeing only Helen in Paul Brent's arms; seeing the fellow's possessive smile as he looked at her; recalling the suggestion of intimacy between them of which, gradually, everyone was becoming aware. Paul Brent was obviously in love with her, and she, equally obviously, was by no means averse to him. And, as Lola said, he could have wangled this job aboard ship for her, so that they could be together . . . Hadn't Helen said he'd recommended her?

And why the devil should I care? David thought furiously. Didn't I put her out of my mind, long ago? Out of my heart, too—*yes, out of my heart!* And she can stay out, for ever. She can marry her handsome ship's doctor, for all I care, and may they be happy together.

But still the ache was there—that deep, insidious ache which refused to be dispelled by anger or determination. Did it mean that her attraction for him was proving as strong as ever? If so, he had to fight it and overcome it. He had to relegate her, this time, very firmly into the past, for that was where she belonged.

Deep in the heart of the ship David could hear the throb of the engines, every beat carrying the *Carrioca* and its passengers nearer to Buenos Aires; nearer to the end of the voyage; nearer to the final parting. When they docked Helen would go out of his life again and this time, he resolved with blind determination, she would go out of it for good.

He himself would see to that.

CHAPTER ELEVEN

Lola Montgomery, clad in a brief bikini, lay sunning herself beside the swimming pool. The cool northern waters were left behind and the first glimpse of tropical sun had brought out a crop of bathers in hopeful search of a tan. Lola was well prepared. She lay upon a towelling rug, with lotions and bottles and a pair of slanting sun spectacles giving her face the mask-like charm of a kitten. With leisurely strokes she oiled her limbs, well aware that every provocative pose enchanted every man within sight.

From the pool she could hear the excited squeals of her daughter as David romped with her. David gave up quite a bit of time to Carol—a little too much, in Lola's opinion. After all, there were other children on board and plenty of facilities for their amusement. But David seemed to have appointed himself as voluntary guardian to Carol.

It was a good sign, of course, and augured well for the future. Lola had great hopes for the future and saw no reason why they should not be fulfilled. David was an attractive man—different from other men in her life. Different from Steve, who had thought of nothing but finance and industry, at both of which he was highly successful. As a husband, of course, he had been overbearing and jealous, resenting her career and her attraction to men. What did he want? she thought resentfully. A little woman at the kitchen sink?

She thrust the memory of Steve aside, for whenever she thought of him she recalled moments best forgotten; the early days of their marriage, before his financial brain became obsessed by big business and her beauty led her into different but equally successful fields. Then they had lived in a little flat in Highgate, modestly, and very much in love. Carol's birth had been a joy to them both and a spur to his endeavour. Nothing was too good for his idolised child. She must have the best of everything, and so must his adored wife.

More and more he stayed in the City, amassing money, while Lola became bored and restless and unhappy. She was not sufficiently maternal to be completely content with a child.

And then she won the beauty competition.

She never knew why she entered for it. Because she was bored, lonely, restless? Whatever the reason, she obeyed an impulse and secretly submitted her photograph. The prize was a sum of money and a film contract.

She didn't really expect to win. When she was summoned to attend the first heat, she went without telling Steve. And so it went on, right through to the final, and then she told him.

He was proud. He bought her a magnificent gown in which to appear and applauded loudest of all. When she won he said, 'Buy yourself something pretty with the money, darling, and hand the film contract back.' And she refused. He thought she would fail as an actress. She didn't.

Within two years their case was in the courts. By then she was well known, not only for her beauty and acting ability, but as a sex symbol exploited by the publicity boys. She had everything she wanted and was wretchedly unhappy.

Not that she admitted it even to herself. This was living. This was what she was destined for. She was never meant to be a humdrum wife in the background of a successful businessman's life.

But when it came to the point she couldn't give up Carol. Why should she? she argued petulantly. She'd done nothing wrong. So the notorious legal battle over the child began, ending in a court decision in the mother's favour which, Lola thought, was only right. What could Steve give the child that she, her mother, couldn't? But, having won Carol, she decided to be unselfish and let Steve have a share in her. So in the sanest and calmest way they compromised on the child's future.

All very civilised and sensible, said Lola's

bright new friends, and wondered who she would marry next. Men came and went in her life, made love to her, bored her. She picked them up, like bright new toys, and discarded them. Actors, producers, film magnates—even an enamoured critic or two, who were always good for a bit of publicity so long as she favoured them. She couldn't understand why she wearied of them all so quickly.

But David Henderson was different. There was a touch of mystery about him which intrigued and fascinated. All that intense reserve, she thought as she watched him behind the dark screen of her sun glasses, was very provoking. The very fact that he hadn't revealed his real name (although, of course, if she had troubled to examine the passenger list she wouldn't have found Keith Hennell amongst it) added to the piquancy.

She saw Sister Cooper approaching, and eyed the girl reflectively. She hadn't a bad figure; not bad at all. Beneath a short white towelling coat, slung carelessly over her shoulders, she wore a swim-suit of plain blue satin—a vivid blue which was a perfect foil for her clear skin and blonde hair.

Helen shed the towelling jacket and dived into the water. When she surfaced her wet hair streamed behind her like golden seaweed. She swam with strong, clear strokes and Lola observed, resentfully, that David was watching her.

Carol let out a squeal of delight and Helen caught her up in the water. The child's legs flayed vigorously, sending a shower of spray over David, who promptly joined in the fun. Quite a merry little trio, Lola thought bitterly, and for the first time in her life she felt excluded, overlooked. And didn't like it.

What has that girl got that I haven't? she though resentfully. Nothing. Nothing at all! She's an efficient nurse, that's all, and not bad looking in her way, but what on earth am I worrying about? I've only to crook my little finger to get all men running, including David, so why should I be troubled by Helen Cooper?

She tried to rationalise her suspicion, but psychological analysis was beyond Lola, whose intelligence was chiefly confined to her acting. She only knew that she was curious about David's previous acquaintanceship with Helen, although there was probably nothing in the world to be curious about.

So Lola dismissed it, turning her attention to Murray Peterson, who lay beside her in the sun. He was a handsome young Apollo, very self-consciously the film star whom all women adored, but he was likeable in his way. He lay upon his side, leaning upon one muscular elbow, watching the swimmers in the pool. The muscles of his back were strong; he was virile and athletic. Beyond his physical virtues there was little to commend him, except an amiability which he could turn on and off like a charm. Being now on show, it was switched on to full power, and so was Lola's. As a pair of leading players they were perfectly suited; a romantic team-up which Mike Saunders had exploited from the beginning. But beyond that they had nothing in common. There was even a sense of rivalry between them, both resenting the other if winning the greater share of praise or attention.

On the surface, however, they were good friends. They had to be. Enacting a love scene with a partner one hated would have been impossible, except for a brilliant actor, and neither Lola or Murray was brilliant. They didn't have to be. The theatre was not their world; it was the film director's talent which made them shine upon the screen.

Murray rolled over upon his chest, the muscles of his broad back rippling impressively, and regarded her with mocking eyes.

'Jealous, darling?'

'Of whom?' Lola retorted acidly.

'The ship's nurse, of course. Our talented author seems more than a little interested in her.'

'Nonsense. They're both fond of Carol, so inevitably they get together when amusing her.'

'That I don't deny, but I observe that beneath his unemotional exterior our author watches Sister Cooper more than she realises. More than *you* realise, also, my sweet.'

'Don't be ridiculous, Murray. And for goodness' sake stop calling him " our author." Keith Hennell is quite brilliant—he's going places, believe me—and so it is only natural that he should be interested in all types of people. They are characters to him, no more.'

'Including that very attractive nurse?'

'Is she attractive? *I* wouldn't know.'

'Oh, yes, you would, darling. You're only too keenly aware of other women's potential rivalry.'

'I don't regard the ship's nurse as a potential rival, if that is what you mean.'

'That is just what I do mean, Lola. And don't pull the wool over your eyes so deliberately. I admit she's not in your class of beauty, but there *are* other types equally attractive to men.'

'If you're trying to be provoking, Murray, you're wasting your time. Why don't you go for a swim? There's a group of adoring fans watching you from the other side of the pool. Jump in, my little performing seal and delight them.'

'My sweet, what a detestable creature you are!'

'My darling, I feel the same way about you.'

He picked up her hand and kissed it

'We've a love scene to rehearse, half an hour hence, so let's scratch each other's eyes out now, shall we, or Mike will wonder why we're not putting our souls into it.'

Lola laughed spontaneously.

'Murray, you're a fool! But mind your own business, will you, as far as Keith and I are concerned?'

'Darling, I couldn't care less about the pair of you but I wouldn't mind making the ship's nurse my business for a while.'

'Then do so,' Lola said eagerly—too eagerly —which brought Murray's quizzical glance back to her.

'So you are jealous, Lola-my-lovely, despite all your protestations. Well, don't let our author know it—or Sister Cooper, either. It's most unwise, I always think, to wear one's heart upon the sleeve.'

'Your audience is waiting,' Lola retorted sharply. 'Don't disappoint it, Murray.'

He laughed, delighted because he had annoyed her. For a long time he had been only too well aware of the admiring little group in the distance, and it pleased him to keep them dallying. Now he rose, flexed his strong muscles, and dived smoothly into the water. A sigh of admiration went up from his fans. When he surfaced he was almost alongside Helen, who was now swimming steadily with David from one end of the pool to the other. She was laughingly challenging him to a race, knowing she was well outstripped, for David was a strong swimmer, his figure every bit as athletic and muscular as the film star's.

Helen hadn't enjoyed herself so much for a

long time; the invigoration of sea air and exercise and the tang of salt water, cold and sharp against her body, was stimulating. It was impossible not to give herself up to the pleasure of the moment, and only in a secret corner of her heart did she acknowledge that this pleasure was enhanced because it was shared with David.

Carol perched upon the side of the pool, her feet dangling in the water, and urged them on. For once, she was carefree and happy and smiling, and when a pallid Agatha Armstrong appeared, the deck steward trailing in her wake with deck chair and rug, the child actually waved to her excitedly and cried, 'Uncle Keith and Helen are having a race— come and watch!' Then she scrambled to her feet and ran to meet the woman, taking her hand with a spontaneous friendliness which surprised her mother as much as it did Agatha.

'So you're up and about again,' Lola said frigidly. 'And about time, too. You've lain in that cabin long enough. You should have come out into the fresh air days ago.'

The timid Miss Armstrong refrained from pointing out that days ago the weather had been wet and windy in the Bay of Biscay, and that anyone who had kept their feet had remained in shelter, and the rest had been in her own condition, full length upon their bunks. She felt too exhausted for conversation, anyway. The walk from her cabin to the

97

promenade deck had seemed like a long safari and now it was over she sank into her deck chair gratefully, feeling guilty at the same time.

Miss Montgomery was out of patience with her, and well she knew it. With the cessation of illness had come the first awakening of fear—fear that when the voyage ended she would be dismissed. Oh, certainly she would be dismissed! Miss Montgomery had already intimated as much. 'I brought you on this trip to be nurse to Carol,' she had said acidly, 'not to be nursed yourself!'

How disillusioning it all was! The thrill of an ocean voyage, life on a luxury liner, association with her favourite film star, all had dwindled into a tight sphere of disappointment.

Helen climbed out of the pool, shaking her wet hair in the sun, then slipped on her white towelling jacket again. 'I must get back to the surgery,' she said. 'Doctor Brent allowed me ten minutes off duty and I'm sure I've overstepped it!'

Her voice was gay and unconcerned. Lola regarded her shrewdly and, for the benefit of David's ears, said, 'You certainly have, dear, but I can't imagine Doctor Brent being cross with *you* . . .'

'Paul is very good natured,' Helen agreed absently. She was watching David as he swung Carol on to his shoulders. Was he playing the attentive father again? The thought made her ashamed. It was obvious that David was genuinely fond of the child.

'So you're on Christian name terms already?' Lola purred. 'I thought medical etiquette demanded the strictest formality between doctor and nurse—or is it more lax at sea?' When Helen made no answer she taunted further, 'I must say you've made good progress with that young man in a very short time, Sister. We've been under way for little more than a week, and this *is* your first voyage with him, isn't it?'

'Yes, it is.'

Before Lola could probe further, Helen coiled her towel turbanwise about her head, waved her hand, and departed. Carol cried, 'Don't go Helen, don't go! Uncle Keith is going to play deck tennis with me—come and join us!'

Helen turned, went back, and kissed the child lightly.

'I've work to do, young lady. I'm not a passenger on this ship, you know!'

'But you *could* come and watch—couldn't she, Uncle Keith? We want her to, don't we?'

David gave Helen a long, level glance. There was a restraint between them now that they had abandoned their carefree enjoyment in the swimming pool. He was remembering so much—too much—and Lola's words still echoed in his ears. *'You've made good progress with that young man in a very short time, Sister.'* She was hinting, of, course. Probing. Trying to

99

find out if it were true that Paul Brent and Helen Cooper were friends of longer standing —and more than friends. And suddenly it was important to him to know for himself, despite his earlier resolve to think no more about her.

Besides, there was Carol. It wasn't going to be easy to avoid Helen so long as the child kept bringing them together. He was genuinely fond of the little girl. He was fond of all children, which was one reason for his distress over the child, Christine Derwent, at the hospital.

As a physician he had quickly realised that Carol's temperamental outbursts were the inevitable result of a deep unhappiness and a sense of insecurity. The child needed help, and he could give it.

So could Helen, he thought suddenly. Carol was already deeply attached to her and that warm maternal instinct which had made Helen such an excellent children's nurse at St. Christopher's could be a great asset now. The sensible thing to do, for Carol's sake, was to put his own personal feelings entirely on one side and seek Helen's aid. There was no need to confide in her—she probably sensed already that Carol was an unhappy child, not a wilful one. Together, unobtrusively, they could infuse a sense of affection and trust into her life.

So what did his own feelings matter? He was adult, self-sufficient, quite capable of living alone, and if not liking it, at least making the best of it. He could write, and write hard, thus suppressing that ever-insistent urge to return to medicine. At the end of the voyage he would say good-bye to Helen, as he had resolved, but suddenly it seemed not only unnecessary but a little ridiculous to try to avoid her in the meantime.

Besides, her association with Paul Brent, however strong or significant it was, was really no concern of his. He had chosen to do what he liked with his own life, so why shouldn't she?

With deliberate logic he argued the case against himself and reached a verdict in Helen's favour, and with the decision came a sudden lightening of his heart. He wanted to see her, to talk to her, to be with her, even if it was only for Carol's sake.

So he said spontaneously, 'Do join us, Helen. I'll take you both on at deck tennis— and beat you!'

'Some other time,' she answered. 'I really am on duty, you know.' She looked down at her wet body and finished with a laugh, 'And I can't appear in the surgery like this—I must dress!'

He swung Carol down from his shoulders and the three of them turned to walk away. Lola watched them carefully. So did Miss Armstrong, who sighed sentimentally—to Lola's extreme annoyance. Goaded, she called,

'Keith, be a darling and bring me my script, will you? I've lines to study. It's on my bedside table . . .'

There was a subtle suggestion of intimacy in the words which caught Helen like a cold shower. David's reaction was completely unrevealing. He said to Carol easily, 'You run and fetch it, Carol—make yourself useful!' and sent the child on her way with an affectionate ruffle of her hair.

'Keith!' Lola called sharply. 'You promised to hear me say my lines.'

'I haven't forgotten,' he answered easily.

Helen turned abruptly, and left them. Fuming, she went down to her cabin. 'Why should I care? Why should I *care?*' she thought furiously as she towelled and dressed.

But she did care. Terribly.

Paul looked up with a smile as she entered the surgery. 'You're late, Sister!' he said with mock severity.

'I know. I'm sorry.'

'Something on your mind?' he asked.

'Not a thing.'

But she didn't speak much for the rest of the morning.

102

CHAPTER TWELVE

Lola picked up the white telephone beside her bed, and asked for David's state-room. She had slept badly so her mood was one of petulance. Ever since she had watched him walking away from her along the deck, with Helen, her mood had been one of illogical suspicion. The fact that she knew it to be illogical didn't help in the least.

She repeatedly reminded herself that Sister Cooper was obviously on very friendly terms with Doctor Brent—more than friendly, if shipboard speculation was justified. Which meant that there was absolutely nothing between her and Keith, and her own jealous apprehension was completely unfounded.

And yet suspicion troubled her like an irritating loose end. She didn't like the way David looked at Helen every now and then, in a deeply personal way which she, Lola, was unable to interpret. Sometimes she would catch him unawares, his inscrutable face revealing nothing, but his eyes watching the ship's nurse in a remote, disturbing fashion. Lola couldn't understand why it troubled her so, for his scrutiny seemed completely detached and impersonal. Nevertheless she was jealous. Intensely so.

She heard David's voice upon the line, and

her heart—which had been unstirred for so long—responded with a surprising intensity. Since she parted from Steve many men had attracted her, but in an unsatisfactory and transient fashion. The more she saw of David Henderson, the more important he became.

'It's a wonderful morning,' she purred. 'How about meeting me at the pool after breakfast?'

'I've had a swim already. At eight a.m. one can have the pool exclusively to one's self. You ought to try it sometime. I suppose you're not up yet?'

She shuddered delicately. 'I'm a lily of the field, didn't you know?' There was a provocative little laugh in her voice.

'A very decorative one,' he admitted.

'Then I shall adorn the sunbathing deck for the rest of the morning, providing you promise to join me.'

'Sorry, Lola. I'm writing solidly until lunch and nothing, and no one, can tempt me away.'

She pouted prettily. It was a pity he couldn't see it, for in the long mirror opposite her bed it looked extremely fetching.

'This afternoon, then?'

'If I get as far as I aim to get.'

'What are you working on? Script revisions?'

'No. The synopsis of a new book.'

'Couldn't it wait?'

'Definitely not. The idea came to me last night and I want to develop it while it's hot.'

He glanced down at the notes on his desk. He had worked on them until the early hours, covering many sheets with his strong handwriting. Assembling them, rearranging them, introducing characters and rejecting others, all this took time; hours and hours of patient deliberation. His years as a physician had developed in him a faculty for intense concentration.

The idea for the book had come to him suddenly as he watched Carol endeavouring, ineffectively, to play with other children. She was difficult, anti-social, confident only when with himself or Helen; with other children— normal children of normal marriages—she was hopelessly out of her depth, conscious of a difference between herself and them, but incapable of understanding it. She was the odd one out, and all her toys, all her pretty clothes, all the indulgences showered upon her by a mother who loved her with a mixture of impatience and adoring pride, did nothing to establish her, as she wished to be established, with her contemporaries. They just didn't accept her.

David's medical career had been devoted to children and suddenly he knew what he had to write—a searching study of an unwanted child, a problem child, an unhappy child. Many had passed through his hands as patients, and now here was little Carol, thrust right into his personal life, becoming increasingly important to him in her need for help. Only one other person sensed this need in her and that was Helen.

He had an urgent desire to discuss his book with Helen, to enlist her interest and co-operation, and to draw upon her experience as a young sister of a children's ward. He could recall innumerable cases they had handled together, cases of sick children whose illnesses were due entirely to emotional disturbance of some kind. In the privacy of her small office, alongside the ward, they would discuss the cases for hours, unaware of time, conscious of a unity of mind which transcended everything else.

'Keith, are you there?' Lola said sharply.

'Yes, I'm here. If I can snatch half an hour sometime during the day, I'll join you.'

It was like a crumb being thrown to a sparrow and Lola was accustomed to a great deal more than crumbs. A petulant retort trembled upon her lips, but instinct checked it. There was something about David which was not like other men, a quality of strength which warned her not to provoke him. Her petulance might bring other men to heel, but not him.

'Well, anyway,' she said with forced lightness, 'I'll see you at lunch.'

'I've ordered it in my room, so that I can work right on undisturbed.'

She took a deep breath. This was *too* much! What was he trying to do—brush her off?

'All right, darling!' she cooed. 'Mike and Murray will keep me company, I have no doubt.'

'So will others,' he laughed. 'I'll see you this evening, Lola.'

'Well, *thank* you, my sweet! Are you sure you can spare the time?'

He heard the sharp slam of her receiver, shrugged his shoulders and went back to work, experiencing no more than a fleeting pity for the woman. She was restless, bored and unhappy, although only he, as a doctor, recognised the symptoms. She had made a hash of her life, despite its apparent success. A hash of her child's, also. And what about her husband? What sort of a man was he? How did he feel about the divorce and, even more important, about the separation from his child? Was he as unaware, as Lola was, that poor little Carol fretted her heart out for him?

David sat for a long time brooding upon the case, his sheaf of notes before him, his pen in hand. He knew the best way to help little Carol—the only way, in fact—and that was to give her a united home with united parents, but such was beyond his power.

Quite suddenly, he remembered his meeting with Helen outside Carol's door, when she had accused him of deputising for Carol's father which, of course, was precisely what he was doing. If it came to that, Helen had been deputising for Carol's mother by looking after

107

her during Agatha Armstrong's indisposition, so perhaps she, too, guessed the real quality of Carol's need. If so, then it was more than ever important to see her, talk to her and, if possible, win her co-operation.

But Helen was restrained and distant with him—friendly upon the surface, but unapproachable beneath. He had lost all sense of intimacy with her; she was a stranger to him now; a stranger in love with another man.

The thought of Paul Brent put a damper upon David's hopes. He was a nice fellow; good-natured, loyal, thoroughly likeable. He was the gay young doctor who should bring happiness into Helen's life and, if Lola's implications were correct, was actually doing so.

How, then, could he possibly hope to get near to her again?

A diffident tap sounded upon his door, then slowly the knob turned and Carol's wistful little face peeped round. She had been watching other children at play, but none had wanted her to join in.

From there she had wandered down to the surgery, but Helen proved to be off duty. After a fruitless search, the child turned instinctively towards David's cabin, feeling a little guilty because she knew Miss Armstrong was searching high and low for her—a stewardess had told her so. 'You're a naughty girl to play hide and seek with your poor nurse,' she had reprimanded severely, which gave Carol an uncomfortable sense of guilt which, in turn, she translated into a resentment against Agatha's vigilance.

'Are you busy?' she asked David timorously.

'I'm never too busy for you, Carol.'

His smile was warm and kind—the smile which had won the hearts of many sick children at St. Christopher's; the smile which had first attracted Helen, too.

'Then could we play deck tennis?' Carol asked eagerly.

David laid aside his pen.

'That sounds a good idea. Let's go!'

At the end of the corridor they came face to face with Helen, just emerging from the hairdresser's. Carol seized her hand eagerly, urging her to join them. 'You *promised* to. Don't you remember? Uncle Keith said he would play against both of us—and you're not on duty now, are you?'

Helen looked at David and smiled spontaneously.

'Is the challenge still on?' she asked.

'Very definitely.'

'Right! Then let's put rings round him, shall we, Carol?'

It was a delightful morning. They played vigorously, thoroughly enjoying themselves, until the deck steward appeared with trays of elevenses, when they flung themselves down thankfully into deck chairs and imbibed long,

109

cool drinks.

When happy and confident, Carol was easy to handle, easy to amuse. After a while she wandered across to a group of children and David and Helen watched as she lingered upon the brink. A vigorous ball game was in progress and she looked on silently, not attempting to push in with her usual aggression. When the ball inadvertently landed at her feet she picked it up quite naturally and threw it back. It was a good throw and a shout of approval went up from the boy who caught it. He did more than that—he threw it back again and before she knew what was happening Carol was joining in the game.

'She'll be all right some day,' Helen said quietly. 'She *will* be all right, won't she, David?'

'Providing life doesn't hurt her any more,' he answered, and found himself suddenly telling Helen about the idea for his new book. It came as easily as conversation with her had come in the old days and for more than an hour they sat in their secluded corner, uninterrupted. Helen's interest was prompt and deep, for the subject was very near to her heart. Relaxed, she lay back, listening to David's deep voice, and it was just as if he had never gone out of her life; as if nothing had changed; as if time had put the clock back and reunited them.

The luncheon call startled them both. 'It

110

can't be that time!' Helen cried, and David, glancing at his watch, remarked ruefully that indeed it was. He had a sense of deep satisfaction and contentment, coupled with a strong reluctance to terminate the moment.

'Thank you for listening to me, Helen.'

'Thank you for telling me about it. The book should be intensely interesting. I shall enjoy reading, it as much as you will enjoy writing it. And what pleases me most of all is—'

'Is what?' he prompted.

'That the background is a medical one. Oh, I know *Strange Destiny* had a medical background, too, but this deals with the one thing in which you were specialising, remember?'

'Of course, I remember.'

'David—wouldn't you consider returning to medicine?'

She put the question hesitantly, fearing a rebuff. None came. That, at least, was something to be thankful for, although the fact that he refused to answer her question troubled her. Instead, he rose abruptly.

'The past is behind me, Helen. Surely you know that there can never be any going back to the past?'

She felt chilled, and could make no answer. She turned to look for Carol and, instead, came face to face with Lola, standing a few yards away, watching them. For one revealing moment Helen saw stark hatred in her eyes.

Then Carol came racing towards them.

'Mummy, *Mummy*! We've had a wonderful morning! Uncle Keith and Helen played deck tennis with me and then I had a marvellous game over there and—Mummy, you're not *listening*!'

Lola jerked round. 'Run along and get ready for lunch,' she said sharply. 'That wretched Armstrong woman has been looking everywhere for you, or says she has.' As the child sped away, her spark of happiness abruptly extinguished, Lola turned and smiled sweetly at David and Helen. 'What a pity she didn't search the sports deck, wasn't it?'

There was a venomous note in her voice which Helen could not understand.

'Perhaps she did, Miss Montgomery, and overlooked us. We could have told her where Carol was.'

Lola's smile was brilliant, but her eyes slid briefly to the sheltered corner in which they had been sitting. It was quite a hideout, she thought viciously. Anyone could have overlooked them there.

'I thought you said you were writing this morning, David?'

Her voice was smooth as silk. Helen could not understand why she wanted to shiver.

'I intended to,' he answered equably, as they turned towards a nearby companionway. 'Instead, I've done even better.'

'Indeed? In what way?'

'I've discussed the idea for my new book very thoroughly with Helen, which proved. more helpful than revising my copious notes.'

'What a helpmate Sister Cooper is,' Lola trilled. 'What would we all do without her?'

David looked at her sharply, then at Helen's slim figure retreating down the companionway ahead. But he said nothing. Lola was tensed up about something and he had a strong desire to shake her. That was the best treatment for such tension as hers, which sprang from resentment and nothing else. She was angry because he had refused to join her at the pool and had then spent his time elsewhere. He gave a mental shrug, irritated by her possessiveness. Then he said, 'You should be grateful to Sister Cooper. She's done a lot for Carol.'

And *I* wanted her to! Lola thought furiously. I thought she'd be useful to me, nothing more. Why on earth couldn't the girl keep in her place? Why couldn't she be nothing more than a nurse in a starched uniform? Why did she have to emerge as an attractive young woman? Because, damn her, that is just what she *is* . . .

Lola's antagonism towards Helen sparked off from that moment, an antagonism which had begun as a diminutive flame and was now fanned into something which threatened to become out of hand; all-consuming;

dangerous. A fire of jealousy which could not be quenched.

She was Helen's enemy now, whole-heartedly. But she would still smile, still pretend—and bide her time.

CHAPTER THIRTEEN

Inspired by his conversation with Helen, David wrote hard all afternoon. Helen was back on duty, to Paul's relief. He had had a busy morning without her. An unexpected case had cropped up—a passenger in Tourist had gone down with a feverish chill, not an unexpected contingency when a ship passed suddenly from cold northern waters into a humid atmosphere. When first setting sail from England head colds and 'flu were usually the order, but when reaching tropical seas ear and throat troubles could begin.

But this case seemed different. It had a feverish quality about it, quite unlike common-or-garden 'flu. Paul described it in detail to Helen.

'Within an hour the temperature had shot up from normal to over a hundred and went on rising. I checked it pretty swiftly, but I'm not so sure it won't rise again. I'm baffled, Helen. It's not quite like anything I've come across before.'

'Tropical fever?' she suggested.

'None of the known ones. Certainly it's new to me. But it's not serious, I'm quite certain. Probably one of the lesser fevers against which passengers aren't normally inoculated. All I hope is that it isn't contagious.'

But by four o'clock that afternoon two more cases were reported, this time in the second class, and just before dinner a first class passenger went down with it.

Paul and Helen ate a hurried meal and returned to the surgery. 'If this thing is going to spread, we've got to nip it in the bud,' Paul said.

But by midnight four more victims were reported.

'There'll be little sleep for us to-night, Helen. We must visit these patients regularly. Whatever he does, a ship's doctor must avert epidemics of any kind.'

'My dear Paul, *you* can't be blamed if an epidemic breaks out!'

'No, but it's my responsibility to see that it doesn't spread.'

'Mine, too.'

He put out his hand and drew her to him. For a long moment he looked down into her eyes. 'What would I do without you?' he said softly. 'I can't imagine how I survived previous trips on the *Carrioca* . . .'

Helen laughed.

'*I* can—with every pretty girl aboard.'

Paul grinned.

'Not with every one, darling. An odd one here and there, I admit.'

'Like Belita?'

'Oh, none so lovely as Belita! She's rare.'

'Ought I to be jealous?'

'I was hoping you would be.'

'I like her too much and I wouldn't blame any man for falling in love with her.'

'Nor I. In fact, if I weren't already in love with you, darling, I could go for that girl.'

Suddenly his arms went around her and he was kissing her passionately. He was young and vigorous and endearing and her heart responded to him.

'Oh, Helen,' he sighed, 'this trip isn't turning out anything like the way I hoped, or expected.'

'What do you mean, Paul? I think everything is wonderful!'

'You know damned well what I mean. I rarely, if ever, have you to myself. Even here in the surgery Wilkins has an infuriating talent for butting in just when I'm hoping for five minutes in which to kiss you undisturbed. And in the evenings we're surrounded by people. That goes for the daytime, too. Helen, we've got to get married just as soon as we reach Buenos Aires. At least then I shall have the nights with you and other men might be warned off during the day.'

She reached up and kissed him gently.

'You're talking nonsense, darling. Other men don't need warning off.'

'I'm not so sure about that. There are quite a few wolves aboard and I've noticed that writer chap hanging round you a good deal.'

She said quietly, 'Surely you don't mean Keith Hennell?'

'If that is what he calls himself, yes. Although I seem to hear him referred to as David.'

'That is his real name—David Henderson. Hennell is his *nom de plume.*'

'I can never understand why writers have to change their names. David Henderson seems good enough to me.'

Good enough to me, too, Helen thought sadly, although she understood well enough David's reason for using a *nom de plume.* Doctor David Henderson belonged to the past —a past which he did not want recalled. Would people have pointed, whispered, or adversely criticised him, remembering 'that case about the little ballet dancer' whose career he had ruined? There was always the risk that someone might recall an incident which he wanted to live down.

Quite suddenly she was depressed, for the past came crowding back with its hope and its heartache, its bewilderment and disappointment. A doctor could do so much for a patient, but no more, and that much was simply his best—always his best. And that was what David had done, fighting for the little girl's life to the best of his ability—an ability far transcending that of many another doctor. But, to David, saving a child's life was not sufficient. Condemning her to a crippled future, as he appeared to have done, was something for which he would never forgive himself.

And yet he had been so confident, so sure that the treatment he prescribed was the right one. Then what had gone wrong? And why?

I suppose we'll never know, Helen thought sadly, and without realising it she let out an unhappy sigh.

'What's the matter?' Paul asked. 'You don't seem yourself to-day. One moment you're up in the air, happy as a lark, and the next you're right down. You were radiant at lunch. What have you been doing?'

'Playing deck tennis with Carol, that's all.'

Why didn't she mention David? Because she was a coward? Because she didn't want to remember the happiness of those hours with him? Or simply because, if she did, Paul would be jealous?

Or was it because she sensed, and respected, David's desire to forget the past? He didn't want it referred to in any way and her sense of loyalty prevented her from confiding in Paul. He would ask, 'Why didn't you tell me you knew him?' and then the truth would come out. And more, perhaps. She might even betray the fact that she once loved David, and to drag up a ghost like that might be dangerous.

So silence seemed the wiser course. Silence, and a determination to look only to the future, which meant marriage to Paul and no looking back whatever.

Fortunately for Helen, who was becoming increasingly aware of a deep sense of unrest within her, she was rushed off her feet with work. She had no time for thought. No time to wonder and speculate about Lola and David. No time to be aware of the film star's increasing antagonism. The fever epidemic increased, some patients recovering rapidly, others more slowly. For three days Paul and Helen searched not only for a cure, but for a preventative. His prescriptions sometimes worked, and sometimes didn't. Anti-bug injections proved either effective, or completely useless.

Feeling utterly weary one day, Helen snatched a brief five minutes alone on deck. It was dusk, and over the vast ocean a pale moon spilt a wash of gentle light, glimmering fitfully upon white-crested waves. It was the hour before dinner, when passengers were changing and decks were deserted and a hush seemed to fall over the ship.

She found an isolated corner and leaned against the rail, lifting her face to the evening air, grateful for even a humid breeze. They

119

were approaching their first port of call. In a few days they would see land and, with luck, this troublesome epidemic would be finally allayed.

She pulled off her starched cap, thinking worriedly that all would be well providing neither she nor Paul succumbed to it. Fortunately doctors and nurses seemed to acquire an immunity to disease, possibly because they daren't allow themselves to give way. Their patients depended upon them too much.

Suddenly she heard approaching footsteps, a man's footsteps, and withdrew into the shadow. She was in no mood for conversation, but to chat with a passenger was a courtesy no ship's nurse could deline. But all Helen wanted right now was to be alone—or with David.

The realisation startled her. Surely she wasn't allowing him to become important in her life again? No, no—not that! She merely wanted to talk to him, to discuss this troublesome epidemic, to draw upon his knowledge and experience as a doctor—even to ask for suggestions and help. If only he could be persuaded to return to medicine—not giving up his writing entirely, but combining the interests. It was obvious, from the subjects he had chosen for his two books, that a medical background still absorbed him.

As if summoned by the power of thought,

120

he was suddenly beside her. The footsteps had ceased abruptly, although she had not been aware of the fact until his voice said, 'Helen?'

She turned, and looked at him out of the shadows. He wore a white tropical dinner jacket and his face looked dark and lean and disturbing. Too disturbing.

'I thought I caught a glimpse of your uniform. If you were seeking seclusion you should have discarded that white overall.'

'That's all right, David. I simply came up for a breath of fresh air—and a bit of solitude, I admit.'

'Then I'm intruding.'

She said, 'No!' very quickly. Too quickly. She bit her lip, with annoyance. Why couldn't she have let him go? Why couldn't she have pretended that she wanted to be rid of him?

Because she wasn't a good liar—it was as simple as that. Because only just now she had been thinking of him, wanting to talk to him again.

He said easily, 'Then how about a turn round the deck? If you're tired, you'll feel better for it.'

She said lightly, 'Thank you, Doctor!' and he gave a rueful smile.

'It's a long time since anyone called me that.'

'They could again, if you wanted them to.'

They were walking along the port deck and it was a full minute before he answered, 'I don't want them to.' He said it with an air of finality which brooked neither argument nor discussion.

So the subject was still taboo, she thought regretfully.

'I hear you're having a busy time,' he said conversationally. 'Is it true that more passengers have been smitten by this bug?'

'Quite true. Most of them recover quickly, but some cases are proving stubborn.'

'Mild cases of fever often do.'

She asked suddenly, 'David, did you ever study tropical diseases?'

'Not intensively. It was children's complaints, as you know, in which I specialised.'

Well, at least, she thought gratefully, he didn't seem averse to discussing the subject.

'Why?' he asked. 'Is something worrying you?'

'It's worrying both Paul *and* me . . .'

The use of Doctor Brent's Christian name didn't escape him. So they had got beyond conventional professional courtesy, he reflected. Not that that was anything to go by in so intimate a set-up as a ship's surgery, run solely by a doctor and nurse. One couldn't expect hospital etiquette to be observed in such circumstances. All the same, she spoke the man's name so easily that David received the strong impression she had used it thus for a long time. The thought troubled him.

'What's the problem?' he asked.

'Just what sort of a bug it is. Paul had to take a course in tropical diseases to qualify for this job, but the epidemic doesn't correspond with any of the known ones.'

'There are an infinite variety, of course. Minor manifestations, too. This is probably one of them—a lesser variation which will simply run the course and clear up, or suddenly respond to prescription.'

'The difficulty is to find the right prescription.' She hesitated, then asked abruptly, 'David, would you be prepared to help us?'

They had reached the stern of the starboard deck. Dusk was rapidly giving place to darkness. A wide companionway yawned ahead of them, leading to the warmth and brilliance below decks. David paused at the top of the steps, obviously determined to end both their walk and their conversation.

'I'm sure Doctor Brent can carry on without any interference from me. He seems to be coping very well. Besides, you're forgetting something. I no longer practise as a doctor.'

That, thought Helen bitterly, was what was known as 'the snub direct.' She turned abruptly and descended the stairs at a brisk pace, her averted back saying plainly what she thought of him.

But she didn't have time to think of him for long, for when she returned to the surgery it was to find Paul sitting before his desk, looking

123

sick and white. His shirt sleeve was rolled up and with shaking hands he was preparing a hypodermic. Helen took it from him, saying firmly, 'I'll do that, and then Wilkins can help you to bed.'

'Can't . . . can't go to bed . . .' Paul muttered. 'Letting you down, old girl . . .'

'You'll let the whole ship down if you try to work in this state,' she reprimanded gently.

'You can't . . . manage alone . . .'

'I won't have to. I've got Wilkins to help me.'

He continued to protest until she promised to find out if there was a doctor amongst the passengers who might give a hand, and when he was finally in bed sank into a state of delirious half-sleep.

'He's bad, Sister. Real bad.'

'Yes, Wilkins. I suspect he knew this was coming and refused to give in. Have you noticed that the patients who ignored the first signs have been hit the hardest?'

Helen studied Paul anxiously. She didn't like the pallor of his skin, nor his raging temperature. Somehow it had never been possible to imagine Paul ill—he was too alive, too robust.

On her way to the purser's office she met Belita. In the whirl of these last days she had not seen her. Belita was looking lovely in a simple dinner dress of acquamarine satin.

The girl paused with her shy, sweet smile.

124

'You look tired, Sister. I hear you are working very hard. The doctor, too.'

'Well, the doctor at least can have a rest now,' Helen smiled. 'The poor man is ill himself.'

She was surprised by Belita's reaction, which was one of deep distress. 'Oh, no!' she cried. 'Is he very bad?'

'Pretty bad. Worse than he need have been if only he had had the sense not to ignore the first signs—but doctors so often do. They have little time to think of themselves.'

'Is there anything I can do for him—or for you, Sister?' Belita added quickly. 'I'd like to help. Of course, I've had no nursing training, but I would do whatever you tell me . . .'

'I wouldn't hear of it, Belita, but thank you, all the same. You go ahead and enjoy the rest of the voyage and keep away from sick passengers. Stay in the fresh air as much as possible, too. Infection is far less likely to attack you there.'

'I don't care about infection! I'd like to do something useful, something practical. I want to *help.*'

Helen was touched, although she suspected that it was really Paul whom Belita wanted to help.

'Thank you, Belita. I may take you up on that offer. Meanwhile I'm on my way to find out whether there's another doctor aboard.' She smiled at the girl gratefully and went on her way.

But she forgot Belita on reaching the purser's office, for there disappointment awaited her. There was only one practising doctor on the passenger list and he had succumbed to the epidemic himself.

'Ah, well!' sighed Helen, philosophically, 'Wilkins and I will just have to cope.'

Uncle Joe eyed her sympathetically. 'Let me know if you need anything. Meanwhile, make good use of the stewardesses. Many are very good nurses.'

'It isn't nursing help I need, Uncle Joe. It's a doctor—and a good one.'

Passing the entrance to the restaurant, on her way back to the surgery, Helen heard a burst of laughter and conversation as the heavy plate-glass doors swung open. Lola emerged, surrounded by her little court of admirers—mostly male—amongst them David. None of them seemed to have a care in the world.

A swift little flame of anger shot through Helen. Beautiful, idle, spoilt, and useless—that was Lola Montgomery. And yet Helen felt that in other circumstances—had she been poor, instead of rich—Lola could have been a thoroughly sound person. Luxury and flattery and adulation had ruined her. If David was prepared to add to that adulation he wasn't the man Helen had once known.

Nor was he the medical man she had

126

known, either. Doctor Henderson of St. Christopher's would never have refused a call for help. Desperate as the need now was, she wouldn't appeal to him again.

Head high, she walked on. Let David hide his head in the sand, let him try to escape the past, let him be enamoured and enslaved by Lola's beauty—what did it matter to her? She had work to do and no time in which to think of anything else.

But in a secret corner of her heart she was aware of an increasing unhappiness and a bitter disappointment.

I'm tired, she told herself sternly. Just tired, that's all.

CHAPTER FOURTEEN

As the purser had said, many of the stewardesses were highly competent, relieving Helen of a great deal of nursing. Nevertheless, she had no time for rest. All the surgery duty fell on her shoulders now and there seemed little hope of a quick recovery for Paul, whose condition grew steadily worse.

She no longer took her meals in the dining-room, but hurriedly from a tray upon her desk. Her absence was observed by David, who had fallen into the unconscious habit of glancing towards her table whenever he entered the restaurant. Although Lola had shown no sign, she was aware of this and resented it. She resented even more David's reaction when, after dinner one night, Belita Cortez said, 'Poor Sister Cooper—she doesn't even come down for meals now that Doctor Brent is ill . . .'

David looked up quickly. They were sitting in the observation lounge, enjoying leisurely coffee and liqueurs. David had been stirring his coffee thoughtfully, but Belita's words cut across his abstraction in a way which didn't escape Lola.

'Brent ill?' he said. 'Since when?'

'The day before yesterday. He went down very suddenly, like everyone else.'

Lola said, 'Thank heaven, I myself am rudely healthy, but I think it a disgrace that the medical staff haven't checked this wretched epidemic.'

'Doctors aren't magicians,' David said a little sharply.

Lola saw Murray Peterson's eyes watching her with amusement. Damn him, she thought furiously. He misses nothing.

His elegant, elocutionised voice remarked lazily, 'It must be pretty hard for Sister Cooper, coping single-handed. I suppose everything falls on her now.'

'That's why she doesn't come down for meals,' Belita said. 'The medical orderly helps, of course, and the stewardesses, and one or two volunteers.'

'Like yourself, darling?' Lola smiled. 'I've noticed you hopping in and out of the surgery once or twice—or was it the cabin next door? Doctor Brent's, I believe . . .'

The girl's face flushed.

'I've been trying to help,' she admitted. 'Not that I'm much good . . .'

'But you try,' David put in kindly. 'That is the main thing, Belita—and more than any of us have done.'

'And how *is* Doctor Brent?' Lola cooed. 'All the better for your ministrations, I'm sure.'

'I'm afraid not. He's been delirious for two days.'

'He sounds in a bad way,' said Murray.

'He is.'

Murray Peterson rose lazily.

'Poor Sister Cooper—a little consolation at a time like this wouldn't come amiss, I think. I wonder if I could deputise for Doctor Brent— and I don't mean medically!'

Lola laughed.

'Murray, you *are* a fool! If the girl is rushed off her feet you don't imagine she'll have time to flirt with you, do you?'

'I can't imagine Sister Cooper flirting with anyone. She's the life-is-real-life-is-earnest type, I fear.'

'Perhaps that is why she makes a good nurse,' David said abruptly.

'*And* why she'll make a good wife for Doctor

129

Brent,' Lola added.

Belita asked, in a voice which strove to sound natural, 'Is it true, then, that she's going to marry him?'

'Well, darling, I wouldn't be at all surprised—would you? Although they're obviously being very cagey about it.'

'Shipboard gossip, Belita— pay no attention to it,' said Murray.

Tears of humiliation stung Belita's eyes. Was her feeling for Paul so very obvious, then? Had everyone noticed it?

Murray took hold of her hands and pulled her out of her chair. 'Come and dance,' he said. 'There's still an orchestra playing in the ballroom and I adore being seen with the prettiest girl on the ship.'

He was gay and kind and his flattery didn't mean a thing. Belita knew that, but was grateful for it at this moment. Lola enjoyed taunting her; she did it deliberately, aiming her poisoned little barbs with deadly accuracy. It amused her to see the girl's naked reaction to the name of Doctor Brent.

David followed them from the observation lounge and accompanied them down in the lift.

'Are you coming to the ballroom, too?' Murray asked amiably. 'Lola won't like that— her court will be depleted.'

'That's too bad,' David answered lazily, 'but I have other things to do.'

*　　　*　　　*

Helen pulled off her cap and ran a tired hand through her hair. It had taken her three hours to do a complete round of the ship, visiting patients in their cabins and others, the more serious ones, in sick bay. She had taken temperatures and given injections and issued nursing instructions to the stewardesses; she had marked charts and made notes and now she was back in the surgery glancing at the list of callers which Wilkins had methodically made. 'I dealt with most of them,' he told her. 'Some were merely suffering from over-indulgence, either in food or drink—the usual complaint after a week of luxury living and idleness!'

Well, at least, thought Helen thankfully, there were no new cases of fever.

'Could you get me a cup of coffee, Wilkins? And make it strong.'

'A good night's sleep is what you need, Sister. If you go on at this rate, you'll drop.'

'No, I won't. A nurse is trained not to.'

When he returned with the coffee, she was sitting with her head in her hands. She looked very young, he thought sympathetically. Too young for all this responsibility. If only Doctor Brent would pull out of it soon, all would be well, but from the look of him that didn't seem likely.

131

Wilkins didn't like the look of Doctor Brent at all. He'd got it bad, real bad, but the orderly decided to let Sister drink her coffee before he told her that. So they sat in silence for a while, aware of the distant throb of the ship's engines, like a great heart thudding below decks, and every now and then distant strains of music from the ballroom. People were actually enjoying themselves, unthinking, uncaring—people like Lola and her little crowd of satellites, Helen thought wearily. And amongst them, David.

The coffee scalded her throat. She was grateful for that, because suddenly there was a lump there—painful and threatening and the hot coffee numbed it. I'm tired, she thought desperately. That's why I want to cry. No other reason.

But the lump persisted. She had to summon every ounce of her self-control to master it. There was no time for tears, no time for thought, no time even to admit loneliness. She had a job to do, and she was thankful for it.

But in the deep recesses of her heart an insidious ache had taken possession, and David had caused it.

'Thank you, Wilkins—that was good. I needed it.'

He took the tray away. Helen rose and adjusted her cap before a mirror. From the door, the medical orderly looked back and said gently, 'You might take another look at Doctor

Brent, Sister . . .'

Something in his voice made her turn.

'Why? Is he no better?'

'I'm afraid not, Sister.'

That means he's worse, Helen thought as Wilkins departed, and went immediately to Paul's cabin.

He lay in a coma, his face beaded with sweat. Her heart was stirred by compassion and anxiety. Poor Paul—he had neglected himself, ignored the symptoms, gone on with his job long after he should have given in. But he was a doctor and what else would a real doctor do?

Unbidden tears came to her eyes. Some doctors could turn their back on things, she thought bitterly. Some could go their own way. And there was David again, filling her mind and her heart with desperate reproach. What had happened to him? Why had he changed? Why should he let one failure embitter him so?

Because he was an idealist and he had betrayed his own ideals, so much so that he could not trust himself, or his judgment again. That was the true answer and it was no use feeling bitter towards him, she thought reasonably. It was impossible for her to do so, anyway, for she knew and understood him so well.

It was very quiet in Paul's cabin. She was aware only of the sound of his quick, uneven breath and the tired beating of her own heart. She stood with her fingers upon his pulse, conscious of a desperate anxiety and need. If only she had *someone* to turn to, someone strong and reliable and dependable. But there was no one. She had to stand upon her own two feet and suddenly they seemed totally inadequate.

The door opened quietly. She turned, and saw David standing there. 'I looked for you in the surgery,' he said. 'Wilkins told me you might be here.'

He came towards her and she observed, with a sense of remote bewilderment, that he was wearing a white overall.

Gently he dislodged her fingers from Paul's wrist, replacing them with his own. She noticed that a stethoscope hung round his neck and, following her glance, he said with a little smile, 'He won't mind my using it, I hope. Naturally, I haven't my own.'

'*David!*'

'May I see his chart?' he asked professionally.

She extended it automatically, her eyes never leaving his face. For a moment he looked at her, then he laid Paul's hand upon the bed.

'You're crying,' he said gently. 'Why?'

She brushed her tears away with the back of her hand. The gesture touched his heart.

'I'm tired, that's all. And bewildered . . .'

134

'About the cases? I can understand that.'

'Not only about the cases. About—this. This moment. And you. What are you doing here, David?'

'Surely it's obvious? I'm in practice again—temporarily.'

A sudden radiance lit her face. Trying to check her joy, she asked, 'Did the captain ask you to take over? Is that why you came?'

'Certainly not. He didn't know I was a doctor—you're the only person on this ship who knew that. I volunteered, Helen. I wanted to. So we work together again—you, and I.'

CHAPTER FIFTEEN

The telephone in David's cabin rang insistently. At the other end of the line Lola listened with gathering impatience. If he wasn't there, where was he? She had searched every bar, every public room, every inch of deck without success.

He had even failed to keep their usual rendezvous for drinks before lunch, and now, in the middle of changing for dinner, she had a sudden urge to speak to him—to know where he was, what he was doing, why he had neglected her. If he had been writing, just where had he hidden himself? There had been no reply from his cabin throughout the day.

There was still no reply.

'I'm sorry,' trilled the telephone operator, 'number two-nineteen doesn't answer!'

Without a word of thanks, Lola slammed down the receiver.

Tears of mortification filled her eyes. The more remote and detached David became, the more she wanted him. His reserve was a challenge, his indifference a spur. 'How *dare* he treat me like this!' she stormed, and swept into the bathroom in a flurry of clinging draperies.

The bathroom was lined with mirrors. She paused upon the threshold, studying her lovely figure, thinking that if only he could see her now he wouldn't be so indifferent.

There was a knock upon her state-room door and she spun round eagerly, hoping it was David. But it was only Agatha Armstrong, looking seedy again. She passed a shaking hand over her damp forehead, muttering indistinguishably. Lola took one look and cried, 'Get out of here! If you're sickening for that beastly fever, get along to the surgery— quickly!'

For reply, Agatha Armstrong slumped to the floor.

Lola ran out into the corridor, shouting for a stewardess. It was a full minute before she found one. 'Where on earth have you been?' she demanded. 'I need you—quickly!'

The stewardess muttered something about

being busy, but hurried after Lola's agitated figure.

'There!' cried Lola, pointing to the unconscious woman on her state-room floor. 'Get her out of here!'

The stewardes was in the bathroom in a flash. A moment later she was moistening Agatha's dry lips, then lifting her head from the floor and forcing it towards her knees. 'She'll be round in a minute, madam, then I'll get one of the stewards to help her back to her cabin.'

'No, no! Not there! She'll pass the infection on to my child!' Lola's hands flew to her face in a dramatic gesture. 'Who knows,' she cried, 'the poor child may have caught it already!'

But Carol was very hale and hearty, appearing in the doorway at that moment and very interested in all that was taking place. '*I* know how to bring someone round from a faint,' she declared. 'I've seen Sister Cooper do it. Did I tell you I've decided to be a nurse when I grew up?'

But her mother wasn't listening. She was on the telephone, saying urgently, 'Give me the surgery, quickly!' But the surgery line was engaged. The stewardess said that wasn't surprising but she'd get word to them right away. At that moment a steward appeared and together they helped Miss Armstrong to her feet.

'We'll take her along to her cabin, madam,'

the stewardess said, 'and then she can be moved to Sick Bay if necessary.'

'But my child! Carol can't share a room with an infectious case!'

'Then I suggest she shares yours, madam,' the stewardess replied courteously.

Carol took a flying leap on to her mother's bed, jumping for joy. 'Goody, goody, goody! I'd love to sleep here!'

Lola rasped impatiently, 'That won't be necessary, Carol.'

At that moment the unfortunate Agatha Armstrong sagged again and was led by the stewardess to a nearby chair. Lola snatched up the telephone receiver, urgently demanding the surgery. When they answered the stewardess politely took the instrument from her hand and began to give details. Lola swept into the bathroom in a whirl of impatience. The sooner the tiresome woman was removed the better, said her expressive back. The door closed sharply behind her.

When she opened it again she stood stock still in surprise, for a doctor was stooping over Agatha Armstrong—a tall man in a white overall, with a stethoscope round his neck. Lola stared in astonishment, for the man was David.

'Keith! What on *earth* are you doing?'

But he made no answer. He didn't even hear her. Carol prattled excitedly, 'He's ship's doctor now—didn't you know? *I* did. Helen

138

told me!'

Miss Armstrong, now revived, was able to stand up and, supported by the stewardess, made her uncertain way from the room. David was following when Lola shot forward and grasped his arm.

'Keith! I've been trying to get hold of you all day!'

'I've been busy. I still am.'

'I'm bewildered, Keith! How can *you* take over from Paul Brent?'

'Any qualified doctor can step in, in an emergency.'

'I didn't even know you were a doctor! You didn't tell me.'

'It wasn't necessary.'

He turned to go, but she waylaid him.

'How did it happen?' she demanded.

'How did what happen?'

She stamped her foot impatiently. 'Why—*this*, of course! Stepping into the breach . . .'

'It was the natural thing to do. The surgery was without a doctor.'

She asked with quick suspicion, 'Who persuaded you? Sister Cooper?'

'No. I volunteered.'

'But did she know you were a doctor?'

'Yes—she knew.'

'So you confided in her, but not in me?'

He turned to the door. 'If you'll excuse me, Lola, I have work to do—'

'Keith—wait! When will I see you?'

'Heaven knows. We scarcely have time to snatch a meal. By the way, Carol should move out of Miss Armstrong's cabin. An extra bed could be put in here for her—there's ample room. I'll see the Purser about it.'

He was gone, leaving Lola in a turmoil of emotion, not least of which was an awareness that David as a doctor was even more attractive than David as an author. He looked so absolutely *right* in that white overall, with the quiet, authoritative air of a medical man. Why didn't I guess? she wondered. Why didn't anyone guess? How else could he have acquired all the knowledge for the background of *Strange Destiny*?

And quick upon the heels of that question came others: Why did he keep quiet about it? Why confide in Sister Cooper, and not in me?

But perhaps the girl found out somehow. After all, she was a nurse. Maybe she had even heard of him before, or knew his name . . .

Lola's memory jerked abruptly, carrying her back to a moment in this very room—the moment of their first meeting. She had introduced them and Helen had said, 'Hallo, David . . .' Just like that. Not 'Hallo, Doctor,' but using his Christian name, intimately, personally.

'Mummy, can I really sleep in here?' Carol demanded excitedly.

Lola ran a hand through her hair and answered absently, 'I don't know, darling—I

140

suppose so, if there isn't a spare cabin. Do run away, sweetie. I want to get dressed . . .'

Carol danced off quite happily. There was a full hour to spare before the children's evening meal was served; with luck, she might find the boy who threw the ball and applauded when she threw it back. He was fun, really. He didn't turn his back on her, as other children did. Not any more. He had even promised to teach her how to bowl.

Alone again, Lola sat down and thought hard. A blind and unreasoning jealousy consumed her. So Helen and Keith had known each other before—she remembered now that they had admitted that. 'Do you two know each other?' she had asked, surprised, and Helen had answered non-committally, 'We've met.' That was all. And Keith added, 'Long ago.'

Long ago. There was an implication about that—a disturbing implication, as if time or fate had severed them and brought them together again. Or am I imagining this? Lola tried to argue reasonably. After all, 'long ago' might mean anything. Long ago when they were on the wards together, or she was a probationer and he a medical student, or merely a doctor and nurse treating the same patients.

Or it could mean, 'Long ago, when we meant a lot to each other . . . knew each other well . . . were important to each other.'

Lola picked up her hairbrush and began to wield it vigorously. To be jealous of a mere nurse was ridiculous, yet jealous she was. Suspicious, too. Indeed, suspicion riddled her unhappy mind like a merciless electric needle. It refused to be still.

Say what he might she was now convinced that Sister Cooper had persuaded Keith to stand in for Paul Brent. Of course, she had! She had gone to him with that sweet, girlish charm of hers and pleaded with him. Oh, thought Lola savagely, banging down her hairbrush so that the array of bottles and jars on her dressing-table rattled furiously, I can just imagine it all! The craftiness of it! The guile! The virtuous innocence! The scheming calculation! All the dice were loaded in her favour and how well she played them!

In their association with doctors, nurses had an advantage over ordinary women. They could meet them on their own ground, talking intelligently upon subjects about which the lay person knew nothing, and then throw in their own personal appeal for good measure. The scheming little hussy! Lola thought viciously. As if I didn't know, ever since the voyage began, that she had her eye on Keith! I've seen her looking at him unawares—remembering, perhaps? Remembering what? Some intimate association with him which she would very much like to renew? I'd put nothing past her—*nothing*!

142

Fury now took full possession of Lola, distorting her reason, twisting every thought, wrongly interpreting every remembered incident. Sister Cooper had got Paul Brent on a string, that was obvious, but it was equally obvious that he wasn't enough for her. She wanted other men, too, and one in particular. Keith.

But she wouldn't get him ! Never, never, *never*! I'll see to that, vowed Lola. *I'll see to that.*

CHAPTER SIXTEEN

Carol felt forlorn. Even sharing her mother's luxurious state-room did little to assuage her loneliness. There wasn't a spare cabin in the entire ship, the purser had informed Lola, so an additional bed in her own apartment was the only alternative. But this didn't please Lola, although it took up such a very small space. She made the best of things, but Carol knew she was not wanted.

Instinct warned her to keep out of her mother's way. Lola's temper was uncertain these days. Carol was also strictly forbidden to go near poor old Armstrong, in case she picked up the infection. What made matters worse was that the parents of other children seemed unwilling to have her around, knowing that her nurse was ill and that she, Carol, might pass on the germ. So now she was absolutely friendless.

She hadn't even Helen to turn to, or David, both of whom were too busy to spare her a moment. Once she had seen Helen hurrying along a corridor and had run after her eagerly, grasping her hand. Helen greeted her affectionately and chatted as usual, but all the time she went hurrying on her way and at the door of the surgery she said kindly, 'Run along, darling—you really mustn't hang around Sick Bay just now.'

David said the same. He was distant and remote, somehow, although his smile was still there and, when he had time to notice her, he was friendly as ever. But nothing was the same. *They* weren't the same, these two people who had come suddenly into her life and brought the first sense of stability and understanding which she had experienced for a long time.

Carol was surprised about David turning out to be a doctor, although it seemed absolutely right, somehow. He was so wise, so kind, so clever. He was easy to talk to and quick with understanding. She didn't have to explain things to him, or try to puzzle things out—he knew, without being told, when she was unhappy or frightened, and sometimes she even felt he knew why, although that was really a secret locked in the deepest corner of her heart. It was hidden away with the memory of

144

her father, like the photograph of him which she refused to have by her bedside.

Lola thought she didn't want it, or had lost it. Anyway, its absence didn't worry her. It proved to her that all the theories about divorce having an adverse effect upon children were nonsense. *Her* child didn't fret for her father—Carol had heard her say so. 'Why, she doesn't even miss him! She had a photograph of him once, but goodness knows what she's done with it now.'

She'd been talking to Murray, sitting in the sunshine on the promenade deck, and Murray had drawled: 'She's thrown it away, probably, and a good thing, too. All that husband of yours was interested in was making money.' Which, surprisingly, had made Lola angry. 'Don't you *dare* criticise Steve!' she had snapped.

Carol remembered the moment quite clearly. She had been playing nearby, apparently absorbed in a solitary game, but all the time she had been listening and watching. It was a habit she had acquired ever since things began to go wrong, because she knew that if she pretended not to listen she would hear grown-up conversation which was not intended for her ears, but which was nearly always about her. She had developed an unnatural astuteness, an instinct far beyond her years. So Murray and Lola hadn't even suspected that she was listening.

Murray had looked at Lola in surprise.

'I must say, darling, that for a woman who has discarded her husband, you're unnaturally swift in his defence.'

'Let's leave Steve out of this, Murray. He's gone out out of my life. Out of Carol's, too, more or less . . .'

How *could* grown-ups be so wrong? Quietly, Carol had slipped away and, from her secret box, which she kept hidden in the locker beneath her bunk, she had taken out her father's photograph and held it to her cheek. When she replaced it the print was wet, and that made her cry more, for a bit at the side of his eyes—where they crinkled up when he laughed—had smudged, so that it didn't look like him any more. But the photograph was still there, locked away as securely as the memory of him, and the longing for him, was locked away in her heart.

The *Carrioca* was well into tropical regions now, but the carefree atmosphere which usually settled upon the ship at this stage of the voyage was missing. There was an increasing awareness that all was not well, that at any moment another passenger might be taken ill; they seemed to go down with the tiresome infection as rapidly as they recovered. Not that all recovered quickly. Poor old Armstrong, who had spent nearly all her time on her bunk since they sailed, seemed likely to remain there for the rest of the voyage and

146

she, Carol, who was wanting to practise nursing (for she was now quite determined to be another Sister Cooper when she grew up) wasn't even allowed near her.

So it was in a mood of frustration and loneliness that her footsteps led her towards the surgery one day. Surely Helen and David would have just a few minutes to spare for her? But when she knocked there was no reply. Timidly, she opened the door. In the dispensary she could see Wilkins busy at a long counter. When he turned and saw her he said, 'What do you want, Missie?' in an absent sort of way, and continued with what he was doing.

'I—I thought Sister Cooper might be here—'

'She's with the doctor on his rounds. Better run along, kid. This is not the place for you.'

'Can't I just watch? What are you doing?'

'Nothing you'd understand. Checking medicines, that's all.'

Carol's eyes surveyed the laden dispensary shelves with awe.

'Are all those jars full of medicine?'

'And more besides. See them drawers over there, all along that wall? Full of drugs, they are. The best, too. The *Carrioca* carries as much as a hospital, take it from me.'

'I'm going to be a nurse when I grow up. I've made up my mind.'

'I should've thought you'd've wanted to follow in your mum's footsteps.'

Carol shook her head vigorously.

'No. I'm going to be a nurse.'

'Well, you could do worse. You'll have to work hard, though. Lots of exams, and things like that.'

'I could start learning now. I could help Sister Cooper! Belita's helping, I know.'

'Ah, the pretty señorita!' said Wilkins with a grin. 'Well, she does her best, bless her pretty heart.'

'Where is she now?'

Carol couldn't understand why Wilkins chuckled as he answered, 'I can't rightly say, but I'm willing to guess. She's self-appointed nurse to Doctor Brent—and why not, sez I?'

'Isn't Doctor Brent better yet?'

'Far from it, poor devil. Got it real bad, he has.'

'Is he in the men's ward?'

'Oh, no, ducks—in his cabin next door. The ward's reserved for passengers and it's full, this trip.' Wilkins passed a weary hand across his forehead. 'I must say, I'll be glad when the voyage is over. The worst I've ever known, that's what it is. Rushed off me blinkin' feet. So's Sister Cooper. She's a wonder, that gal.'

He turned his back upon Carol and, aware that she was dismissed, she crept away. But outside in the corridor she paused. Upon the adjoining door was a neatly printed notice: 'Doctor Paul Brent, M.D., B.S.' She knew what the letters stood for, because Helen had

148

explained once. Doctor of Medicine and Bachelor of Surgery. Would he still be a bachelor when he married Helen? she wondered. Because he *was* going to marry Helen, or so said Miss Armstrong, although Carol couldn't see how she knew. 'But it's obvious!' Agatha had sighed. 'And so romantic!' But Carol couldn't see that, either. She had never taken to Paul so much as to David. He was nice, of course, but he never had time to spare for herself. Once she had even heard him refer to her as 'a spoilt brat' and she had hated him for it.

But now, overcome by curiosity and loneliness, she opened his door. She didn't really know why. It was simply an instinct which she obeyed. Perhaps Belita would be there—pretty Belita, who wore all those lovely clothes, and who seemed utterly indifferent to Murray Peterson, who ran after her a good deal. But Murray, of course, ran after all women who didn't run after him. They were the ones he wanted, Lola said. If they lined up adoringly he just wasn't interested in them. They were nothing but an admiring chorus which he took for granted. But a woman who didn't want him was a challenge.

Funny people, grown-ups, thought Carol sagely.

Except Helen and David and her own father . . .

And thinking thus she tiptoed into Paul's

149

cabin.

He lay very white and still, and quite alone. His eyes were closed and he was breathing in a funny way. His forehead was moist, so Carol picked up a towel and wiped it gently. He didn't even stir. Was he asleep, or dying? she wondered with interest. She didn't want him to die, even though he was impatient with her sometimes.

He stirred and muttered something indistinguishable, tossing restlessly from side to side. A breeze fanned the chintz curtains which were drawn across the portholes to cut off the scorching tropical sun. An electric fan whirred silently above his head. The room was cool and air-conditioned, but he looked awfully lonely lying there.

There was a handkerchief lying on the floor. beside his bunk. Carol stooped and picked it up. It was a pretty handkerchief—a lady's—small and lace-edged. It had an initial embroidered delicately in one corner the letter B. B for Belita, she thought—Doctor Brent's self-appointed nurse. That was what the medical orderly had called her, although Carol wasn't really sure what a self-appointed nurse was.

Gently, she wiped Paul's forehead again, puzzling over the word as she did so. Self-appointed. That meant appointed by yourself, didn't it? But what did 'appointed' mean? She gave that one up, turning back more willingly to her own childish reasoning. Surely it only meant that you'd made up your mind to be a nurse, and so became one? It was as simple as that. And if Belita had done it, so could she.

Carol's young face lit up suddenly. What a *wonderful* idea for a game! But something better than a game, more than a game! It could be real, and happen right now!

In a flash, she tied the towel around her waist, surveying herself in a mirror with approval. It looked just like an apron—a nurse's apron. But alone, it wasn't enough. She had to have a cap of some sort. So she snatched anther towel from beside the handbasin and draped it about her head. It looked a bit like a nun, but with a stretch of imagination it could be a nurse's headdress. And anyway, weren't nuns sometimes nurses, too?

Firmly, she knotted the towel behind her neck, feeling suddenly grown-up and happy. Now *she* was a nurse. Not only did she look like one, she felt like one. Moreover, she knew how to behave like one. And the first thing she had to do was to take her patient's temperature and feel his pulse . . .

So she stooped over Paul Brent with concern; lifting his wrist, which proved to be surprisingly hot and moist. But she didn't know where the pulse was situated and couldn't feel a thing. Was he dead? she thought with childish wonder. That meant he

151

wasn't breathing, didn't it? And the only way to find out was to stoop close . . . close to his mouth . . .

She could feel the uneven fanning of his breath upon her cheek. 'So you're not dead!' she commented with delight. 'Then I'll make you well again!'

The door opened, but Carol didn't hear. She was too absorbed in her new and wonderful game. Not until Helen's voice said sharply, *'Carol!'* did she jerk to awareness.

Helen was at her side in a flash, seizing her hand and drawing her quickly out of the room. Carol let up a wail.

'I was nursing him! I was going to make him well! *Please*, Helen, don't be cross!'

'I'm not cross, darling. I just want you in the surgery for a minute . . .'

Things happened quickly then—so quickly that Carol had no time for further protest. Helen perched her upon the doctor's desk and rolled up her sleeve. Carol watched in bewilderment, too awed to question. She wasn't frightened, because Sister Cooper was calm and kind and not fussing in the least, so Carol was merely curious as to what was going on and why she had been swept out of Doctor Paul's cabin in such a hurry.

Helen walked briskly into the dispensary. Wilkins was no longer there. Carol could hear her moving quickly, opening and shutting that big thing they called the sterilizer. Spurred by curiosity Carol jumped down from the table and reached the dispensary door just as Helen turned from the dispensing counter with a kidney bowl in her hand, covered with a cloth.

She smiled at Carol and said, 'Back on to your perch, young lady!' But despite the unhurried tone of her voice there was a sense of urgent command which the child instinctively obeyed.

Helen was cleansing a small area of Carol's arm when the door opened and David walked in. His perceptive glance passed from Helen to the child and back again.

'What has happened?' he asked quietly.

'I found her in Paul's cabin, pretending to be a nurse . . .'

'I was only playing!' Carol protested.

'I know you were, darling. It was a nice idea for a game, but Doctor Paul is very ill and we must make sure that you won't be, too.'

Helen removed the cloth from the kidney bowl and picked up the hypodermic.

'What's that?' Carol asked with interest.

'It's something you will use if you become a nurse one day. It makes people well when they are ill and helps to prevent them from becoming ill when they are well.'

'Does it hurt?'

'Not if it is used properly. Then it merely gives a prick which is over in a minute.'

Carol's mouth began to quiver. For the first time, she was frightened.

David laid a reassuring hand upon her head. 'That's a handsome headdress, isn't it, Sister? She'll make a real nurse one day, won't she?'

Carol's lips stopped trembling. 'That's better,' said Helen. 'That's how a real nurse has to behave, always.'

Above the child's head Helen's eyes met David's.

'Ready, Doctor?'

He looked at her in surprise. It was her job to administer injections, but now she held the syringe out to him.

'I'll hold your arm, Carol, and the doctor will give you the teeniest prick and then it will all be over.'

Take it, her eyes said to David. Take it. It is your job; it is up to you. Suddenly she knew that it was important that he should do it. It was a test, a challenge to him, even though it conjured up memories of the past, carrying them back to a moment long ago when she had held a small girl's arm whilst he administered an injection. It was important *because* it recalled the past . . .

The moment was tense, uniting them like a strong, invisible current. Automatically, David reached out and took the syringe. His fingers touched Helen's just as on that other occasion, and all of a sudden the horror of it came rushing back into his mind. He had failed then. Failed utterly.

The moment, though brief, seemed an

eternity. Helen knew what he was thinking and feeling. They were mentally atune, just as they had been in the past. She said quietly, 'Ready, Doctor?'

'Ready, Sister.'

He turned to the child. Helen held the little arm gently, but firmly. Even so, Carol began to whimper.

And at that precise moment the door burst open and there was Lola, staring at them aghast.

'What's going on here?' she demanded, and swept dramatically towards her chid. 'My darling, what are they doing to you? Why are you here? I've searched absolutely *everywhere* for you . . .'

She was about to seize Carol when Helen's restraining arm intervened. 'Keep away, Miss Montgomery, please!'

Lola flung her aside.

'What are you doing to my child?' she demanded, then, seeing the hypodermic, let out a little shriek which had the immediate result of making Carol dissolve into tears.

A flicker of anger lit David's eyes.

'Sister, get her out of here. You can come back, Lola, when we've given Carol the injection—'

'An injection! What for, in heaven's name? She's not ill!'

Helen said, 'We want to make sure she won't be,' and urged the woman towards the

155

door. But Lola rounded on her furiously.

'You're not going to hurt my child! I won't let you hurt my child!'

Carol's sobs became a wail—loud and turbulent and frightened. Now Helen felt angry, too.

'We're not *going* to hurt her! But we've got to take precautions—'

David interposed in a brisk professional voice, 'Helen found her next door, stooping over Doctor Brent. She was pretending to be a nurse. As Helen says, we've got to take precautions. Now go outside, please—you're frightening the child.'

But Lola was suddenly beside herself.

'Who allowed her to go in there?' she stormed. 'Sister Cooper, I blame you for this!'

'That's ridiculous!' David exclaimed impatiently.

'And I suppose it is ridiculous to suggest that a nurse is inefficient if she allows a child near a highly infectious case?' Lola raged.

'I tell you, Helen didn't even know the child was there!'

'She must have wandered in of her own accord,' Helen put in helplessly.

'And you let her!'

'How could I prevent her? I was on the wards . . .'

'Then you should have locked Doctor Brent's door!'

'And you,' Helen replied icily, 'shouldn't

156

allow your child to roam the ship at will—not when there's an epidemic aboard.'

She turned back to the child. The injection had to be given quickly. But Carol, infected by her mother's panic, fought like a little wild cat.

Lola's voice rose shrilly.

'And who is responsible for the epidemic, I'd like to know? *You,* Sister Cooper! You should have prevented it in the first place. You exposed my child to infection and I'll see that you're punished! I'll report you to the shipping line! I'll see that they never employ you again! My God, I'll get even with you for this!'

For a split second David's penetrating eyes stared at her, seeing her, for the first time, as she actually was. 'You're beside yourself, Lola,' he said quietly.

Laying down the hypodermic he took hold of her shoulders, turned her round, and led her firmly out of the surgery. Then he locked the door and returned.

Helen picked up the syringe and handed it to him again and in a detached corner of his mind David observed that her hand trembled imperceptibly. But now there was no time for thought, no time for words. They had to work fast.

Once more Helen took hold of Carol's arm and this time David gave the injection. It was over in a moment. The child's sobs subsided into mute surprise. There was an abrupt silence in the surgery, but Lola's screaming

157

accusations still lingered in the air. David looked across at Helen and saw the glint of tears behind her eyes. She picked up the kidney bowl and syringe and, turning abruptly, went back into the dispensary, her averted back discouraging any comment.

David crossed to the door and opened it.

'You can come in now, Lola.'

His voice was strictly professional, hiding his secret anger. He felt that he would never forgive her for threatening Helen, or for accusing her unjustly, but it was his job, as a doctor, to hide his thoughts.

She looked distraught and anxious, and his voice softened.

'Carol will be all right, my dear, and I assure you we didn't hurt her.'

In the dispensary Helen stood quite still. The concern in his voice didn't escape her. It was concern for Lola, of course. He was talking to her now with gentle sympathy, the way a man talked to a woman he cared about. It didn't matter to him that Lola had been cruel and unjust to herself. He excused all that, as a man excuses everything in a woman he loves . . .

CHAPTER SEVENTEEN

Helen pulled herself together and went on with her work. In a busy nurse's life there was no time for introspection or self-pity. In any case, she argued forcefully, why should she feel sorry for herself? David meant nothing to her any more. She was engaged to Paul and for that she should be thankful. There was nothing complex or deeply emotional about Paul; nothing disturbing; nothing dynamic. He was sweet and kind and always the same; cheerful, inconsequent, and gay. He would never break her heart. It was the brilliant men, like David, who could tear a woman to pieces.

So Lola was welcome to him. Let *her* be tormented by him. Let *her* try to guess what was going on in his mind or in his heart. She, Helen Cooper, had a happier future to look forward to—a future as Paul's wife. It would be serene and untroubled and companionable, so what more could a girl ask?

A great deal more, common sense whispered. A very great deal more. Mental affinity for one thing. Mutual passion for another. The one grew out of the other, so if, to start with, the affinity of mind was merely companionable, how deep would be the passion?

She evaded that one. The question was too

disturbing—even frightening. She had made a bargain with Paul and she intended to stick to it.

But could one bargain with love?

The thought pulled her up with a jerk. She was face to face with something she didn't want to see, because it was safer to pretend it wasn't there. But reality has a way of forcing itself upon a person, catching them unawares, and right at this moment that is what it did. Face the issue! it cried. Stop pretending! You're fond of Paul, very fond, but that is all. Be honest with yourself.

Helen stared unseeingly at the charts upon her desk. She was alone in the surgery. Wilkins had gone off duty for a couple of hours and David—where was David? She really didn't know. After giving Carol the injection he had taken the child by the hand and, with Lola, left the surgery. He hadn't even glanced into the dispensary, where Helen was fighting her own private battle with tears.

Well, at least he had not intruded upon a moment which was intensely private, intensely personal. To have betrayed her feelings to him would have been unbearable.

She pulled herself together with an effort and continued to study the charts. On the whole, they were favourable. Six more patients to-day had recovered and several more were showing a decided improvement. To counterbalance these a few new cases had occurred, but proportionately less, which indicated that the epidemic might be gradually subsiding.

And if *that* doesn't answer Lola's unjust accusations, thought Helen furiously, I don't know what will!

The film star's threats still lingered in her ears. They had been wild and incoherent, prompted by panic, but their underlying viciousness revealed an intense determination. 'I'll get even with you for this!' she had declared, and she meant it. And yet Helen could not believe that her enmity was solely on account of Carol. There was an underlying reason which was baffling.

Suddenly Helen remembered the look of hatred upon Lola's face when she had come in search of her child and found herself and David alone together in a corner of the sports deck. That had been a wonderful morning, alive with understanding and warm with hope, for it had been an echo of moments shared with David long ago, when a sense of affinity had united them. But with Lola's coming it had been shattered, just as that moment in the surgery had been shattered just now.

She hates me, Helen thought calmly. For some reason, she absolutely hates me. But why? I've done nothing to hurt her.

She sighed, and put away the charts. Introspection and worry would get her nowhere. Besides, she had work to do.

161

Meanwhile, a spot of lunch wouldn't come amiss. She was about to ring for the steward when the door opened and David returned.

There was an air of satisfaction and well-being about him. To what was it due? Helen wondered spontaneously. To the fact that he had been with Lola, comforting and reassuring her, or to a feeling that he had done a job and done it well?

To her surprise he came over to her and put his hands upon her shoulders. Looking down into her eyes he said, 'Thank you, Helen.'

'For what?'

'For making me give that injection. For making me face up to a moment which, briefly, I shunned.'

She felt a warm tide surge upward from her heart, like a fountain overflowing.

'What made you do it?' he asked softly. 'What made you know that it was important, essential, imperative to me?'

'I just knew,' she answered simply. 'I felt that here was a chance to make yourself *prove* yourself *to* yourself.'

His hands still upon her shoulders, he continued to look down at her. There was a little smile upon his lips and in his eyes an expression she could not fathom, but suddenly, beneath it, her own glance fell. She turned her head away. She wanted to move from his grasp, but could not. She wanted to speak, but no words would come. And much, much more

162

than that she wanted to drop her head upon his shoulder and feel his arms go about her . . .

The desire was terrifying, and when he said softly, 'How well you understand me, Helen—but then, you always did. We understood one another instinctively, didn't we?' She could bear it no longer. With one violent movement she jerked away from him.

'Helen, what's the matter?'

'Nothing! Nothing!'

She pressed her finger upon a bell-push, summoning the steward urgently.

'I need some food,' she said briskly. 'How about you, David? Have you eaten?'

'Not yet. But I don't know that I approve of these snacks-off-a-tray in which you're indulging these days. It would do you more good to have a proper meal.'

'I don't need one. An omelette and coffee will do me very well.'

The door opened.

'You rang, sir?'

'Omelettes and coffee for two,' David told the steward.

'In here, sir?'

'In here.'

'No time to eat properly to-day, either?' the man asked in concern.

'With luck, we'll dine tonight,' David told him.

When the door closed, Helen said, 'There's absolutely no reason for you to have a scratch

163

meal just because it is all I want. Why don't you join Lola in the restaurant?'

'Why should I?'

She had a thousand answers to that, and stifled them all. To avoid replying she began to file the charts with meticulous concentration. She could feel David's searching glance upon her, but refused to meet it. After a few moments' silence he said abruptly:

'Helen, I want to talk to you.'

'About what?'

'Lola.'

'I see.'

'I don't think you do. You're worrying aren't you, about those stupid threats she made? Please, don't. She was overwrought and has probably forgotten, by now, that she ever uttered them.'

Helen took a deep breath, turned, and faced him.

'*She* was overwrought? Must an idle passenger be the only one to enjoy such a privilege?'

'Helen!'

'Well—must she?' Helen was aware that her voice was rising tautly, but could do nothing to stop it. 'Can't a nurse be a human being, as well? Can't *I* indulge in tiredness or even hysteria, if I so wish? No, of course not! I'm Sister Cooper, ship's nurse, calm in the face of every crisis—or heaven help me!'

She slammed the file shut, ashamed of her

164

outburst but not in the least sorry. It was the Lolas of this world who received all the sympathy and the Helens who were expected not even to need it.

There was an abrupt knock upon the door and the steward entered bearing a laden tray. Helen turned to a corner wash-basin and began to scrub her hands vigorously. Not until the door closed did David speak and the note in his voice was one of amused compassion.

'Come and sit down and get yourself outside this omelette before it turns to leather.' Taking hold of her shoulders he turned her round, pulled the towel from her hands, and forced her into a chair. 'And while you eat it you can listen to me, for a change.'

'Then your omelette will turn to leather, too.'

'I can eat as I talk.' Suiting action to words he began to do so. 'I don't blame you for blowing your top. If there's anything else boiling up beneath it, go ahead and erupt further. It will do you good.'

Helen smiled ruefully. 'That's the lot, I promise.'

'In that case, you can listen to me. Pay no attention to Lola's temper just now—she didn't mean a word of it.'

'No?'

He looked at her, observing the sceptical expression upon her face. He had never seen Helen look like that before, and it disturbed

165

him almost as much as Lola's fury. But he was more surprised by Helen's brief outburst, for it was more out of character. Helen, thank goodness, had never been sugary-sweet, but she had never been cynical, either.

She's tired, he thought gently. Dog tired, poor girl. And no wonder, the way she's been slogging these last days. There was more excuse for her than for Lola, who needed little provocation to fly into a temper. Nevertheless her concern for her child had been genuine enough—the first sincere concern she had revealed for little Carol—and that he took to be a good sign. Carol badly needed a mother's care. A father's, too . . .

He said to Helen, 'She was grossly unfair to you, I admit—'

'Thank you,' said Helen politely.

'But make allowances for her state of mind. She was shocked when she saw us standing over Carol with a hypodermic.'

That's right, thought Helen furiously, make excuses for her! To check an angry retort, she said precisely nothing.

'The truth is, Helen, that Lola is really a very unhappy woman.'

But *you* will make her happy! Helen thought wretchedly, and wondered why she wanted to cry.

David's hands reached out and covered hers. 'Helen, listen to me. I'm positive Lola won't attempt to make trouble for you—why

166

should she?'

Because she dislikes me, Helen thought, and again kept silent.

'In any case,' David continued, 'I would see that she didn't.'

'You?' Helen asked tautly. 'How? By persuasion, or command? I imagine she would yield to either, from you.'

He looked at her with a kind of puzzled surprise.

'By neither,' he answered. 'Everyone, from the captain downwards, knows how hard you and Brent have worked to check this epidemic. Do you think any of us would allow any criticism, or permit anyone to suggest otherwise? I can understand your anger, but what else has got into you? *Something* has. You're not yourself.'

'Oh, yes, I am!' she retorted heatedly. 'For the first time since you knew me, perhaps, I am being completely myself! And that means fire, not water! Heat, not ice!' She put a hand to her forehead and began to laugh. 'Don't look like that, David—so utterly surprised!' She rose, pushing back her chair so sharply that the chain which anchored it jerked to an abrupt halt. This had the undignified and slightly comical result of making Helen sit down again abruptly.

'Good,' said David calmly. 'That keeps you here a moment longer.'

'But only a moment. I have work to do.'

'We both have work to do.'

'Then don't you think we'd better get on with it, or do you still want to plead Lola's defence?'

'To hell with Lola!' he burst out furiously, and to Helen the words were music in her ears. 'Oh, Helen, *Helen*—can't we find one another again?'

She sat very still. Even her heart seemed to stop beating. Anger, jealousy, hysteria, all evaporated beneath an overwhelming sense of happiness.

'What did you say, David?' she whispered.

For answer he came round to her, pulled her to her feet, took her in his arms and kissed her. It was a long, lingering kiss, suspending them both, for an exquisite moment of time, at the heart of the universe. About them, heaven and earth stood still.

When at last he drew away, David laid his cheek against her own. Neither spoke. Helen closed her eyes and surrendered all thought to the sheer delight of feeling. His nearness, his strength, his very existence stirred her to the core of her being.

He kissed her again, this time with increasing passion. Instinctively, she responded. Desire leapt between them and all the longings and the loneliness of their separation dissolved beneath their joy.

There was a sound from beyond the wall; from Paul's cabin. His voice rose inarticulately, bringing Helen back to reality with a sudden shock. She jerked away from David, thrusting him aside almost violently, and without looking at him she stumbled from the room.

Paul! she thought. *Paul!* What have I done?

CHAPTER EIGHTEEN

Paul lay upon his back, his eyes open. His head moved restlessly from side to side. Helen felt a sudden access of pity and shame. Although his eyes were open, he was not aware that she was there.

After a moment she overcame her emotion, resorting once again to her professional training. She took his temperature, felt his pulse, and was entering the details upon his chart when David entered.

'How is he?' he asked. Like herself, he was once more impersonal, efficient, unemotional.

'About the same.'

'Let me take over, Helen. You go and rest. You haven't had an hour off duty since the early hours.'

She turned without a word, refusing to look at him, but only too well aware that he was watching her and that his glance was questioning and compelling. Was he wondering why she had turned away from him so blindly, so violently? If so, he would never know the reason. Never. Never.

Alone in her cabin she shed her uniform, slipped into a cotton housecoat and lay down upon her berth. But sleep was out of the question. She was too deeply disturbed, too emotionally upset. The touch of David's lips still lingered upon her own. The remembrance of his kisses was an ecstasy in her blood—an ecstasy which Paul had never awakened and never would awaken now.

I can't marry him, she thought clearly. It is quite impossible. It wouldn't be fair to him and as soon as he is well, I must tell him. It is the only honest thing to do.

And with that thought, surprisingly, she fell asleep. The deep sleep of exhaustion took full possession of her until she was awakened by an urgent knocking upon her door.

She was surprised to discover that she had slept for four hours. 'Doctor Henderson said you weren't to be disturbed,' the agitated stewardess told her, 'but it's that little girl Carol—she's asking for you, Sister—'

'Asking for me?' Helen repeated, shedding her housecoat and scrambling into her uniform. She was still a little befogged by sleep and had to dash cold water repeatedly on to her face to dispel it.

'Crying out for you, she is, Sister . . .'

'You mean she's ill?' Helen demanded sharply.

The woman nodded. 'And *is* that mother of

hers in a state! Threatening to sue the line and goodness knows what! Anyone would think the child was the only sick patient aboard . . .'

'Where is she? In the children's ward?'

'Oh, no, Sister—her mother won't allow her to be moved. Seems to think she'll die!'

Helen pushed past her and hurried to Lola's state-room. As she entered Lola spun round and cried, 'So there you are at last! Why didn't you come before?'

'Because I gave orders that she was to be left undisturbed,' said David's voice.

He was standing beside Carol's bed, examining the restless little figure, but over his shoulder he finished, 'Sister Cooper hasn't had a decent night's sleep for days. She can't go on indefinitely, like a machine.'

'Helen . . .' Carol muttered unintelligibly. 'Want . . . want . . . Helen . . .'

'I'm here, darling.'

Helen took the hot little hand in her own. Above the child's head, her glance met David's. She saw disappointment in his eyes, a deep disappointment, and for a moment she thought: Surely he doesn't blame himself for this? Surely he doesn't regard *this* as failure, too?

Her heart lifted when he smiled at her, for it was no longer the bitter smile with which she had become familiar during the voyage, but the smile he had given her in the past, when they worked side by side on the hospital wards.

171

Yet even at this moment she sensed a deeper, more personal quality, and her heart was stirred.

Behind her, Lola sobbed, 'You see what a stupid waste of time all that injection business was? Oh, David, why did you *do* it? You hurt her, you hurt her!'

David turned and said gently, 'It had to be done, Lola. It was a precaution which failed because it was applied too late.'

Lola burst into tears. It was the first time she had ever seen her child ill, apart from a bout of German measles which a proficient nurse had brought her through. And then, of course, there had been Steve to lean on. He had been a tower of strength, reassuring his wife that it was nothing more than a childish complaint—which, indeed it was. Carol had taken it in her stride and soon been up and about again. But this was different. Now she was delirious, not knowing her own mother, wanting only Helen Cooper whom she, Lola, now hated. The fact that Carol could only be soothed by the ship's nurse inflamed her mother's jealous mind.

Carol's temperature had soared rapidly and alarmingly, but Lola took no consolation from David's assurance that childish temperatures were usually swift and high, capable of subsiding just as quickly.

'If you hadn't let her go into the doctor's cabin,' she hurled at Helen again, 'this would

172

never have happened!'

David said sharply, 'That isn't true, Lola. Carol could have picked up the germ before she ever visited Doctor Brent—indeed, she must have done, for it couldn't have developed so rapidly otherwise. Don't forget she had been in close contact with Miss Armstrong right until the time the unfortunate woman was taken ill herself.'

'Damn Agatha Armstrong! *Damn* her! She's been nothing but a nuisance to me ever since I engaged her! I'll get rid of her at the end of the voyage, and no mistake!'

Carol's murmurings had subsided and, at a brief signal from David, Helen took charge of Lola, who was now sobbing hysterically.

'We'll take every possible care of Carol,' she said gently as she persuaded the harassed woman to take a sedative. 'If you'll agree to her being moved into the children's ward she will be more easily accessible for us. It's just along the corridor from the surgery . . .'

'I won't, I won't! She must stay here, with me! Oh, God, don't let her die! She's all I have left!'

A deep pity welled up in Helen's heart. Perhaps David was right, after all, when declaring that Lola Montgomery was really a deeply unhappy woman. More than unhappy. Lonely, perhaps. The terrible loneliness of a woman who searched eternally for love, and never found it.

Urging Lola to lie down, Helen returned to Carol. The child was absolutely quiet now, and appeared to be sleeping. That was a good sign, indicating that her attack might very possibly be a mild one. David said, 'I'll be in the surgery if you want me, Helen,' and after a brief glance at Lola, who was sobbing spasmodically into her pillow, he departed.

Helen did what she could for Carol and, once assured that both the mother and child were asleep, she closed the door quietly and departed.

'I wish Lola would agree to Carol being moved,' she said to David as she re-entered the surgery, 'but in her present state of panic, persuasion would be useless.'

He looked up, nodding agreement. His face was tired but even greater than his tiredness was his disappointment. So his reassurance to Lola had been mere words, Helen realised.

She said spontaneously, 'David, surely you're not blaming yourself because the injection was too late? It is absolutely true that the child could have contracted the infection earlier. And it must have been very much earlier, to have manifested itself now.'

'I know, but all the same I'm disappointed.' His mouth tilted wryly. 'It's even ironical, isn't it? That I should fail again, I mean.'

'But you haven't failed! If I had given Carol that injection the result would have been the same!'

174

'I suppose you're right,' he answered wearily, but the shadow of little Christine Derwent seemed to hover between them, so much so that Helen said spontaneously,

'David—*David*! Can't you forget?'

'Never,' he answered abruptly. 'I can never forget.'

She had unconsciously held out her hands to him, but now they fell shakily to her sides. Would the wound in his heart never be healed? she wondered desolately. Was there nothing she could do to erase it?

A sense of bleakness touched her. A short while ago she had been in his arms; he had kissed her with passion and desire; they had existed for one brief and exquisite passage of time upon a plane of happiness such as they had never attained before, yet now he was beyond her reach again—remote and untouchable.

She turned away. His voice followed her. It was clipped and abrupt. 'I suppose I ought to apologise,' he said.

'For what?'

'For a moment of madness. For kissing you as I have always wanted to kiss you.'

Her heart trembled. The trembling spread to her hands, betraying her. She thrust them into the pockets of her starched uniform, the better to control them.

'Well,' David said harshly, 'I *don't* apologise, even though you did flee from me as if I were

175

the devil incarnate.'

She looked at him with a tremulous smile, a longing for him rising within her so intensely that in another moment she would have flung herself into his arms, begging for his lips upon hers, but at that moment the surgery door opened and Wilkins marched in, whistling cheerily.

The sound was a discordant one, severing the moment.

Wilkins said cheerily, 'The pretty señorita is approaching—hoping to nurse her favourite patient again, I reckon!' and with a wink and a nod over his shoulder he disappeared into the dispensary.

A minute later Belita appeared in the doorway. Despite her close proximity with the patients and, as Wilkins suggested, one in particular, she had remained immune from the fever. She looked radiantly healthy. Having marched round the deck six times, a health hint passed on to her with great insistence by Helen, she now had a gentle rose tint in her amber skin.

'I've come to report for duty,' she said with a smile, adding in the same breath, 'How is Doctor Brent?'

'I'm just going to visit him,' Helen told her. 'Coming?'

David watched them depart. Helen suddenly seemed very remote and detached, quite beyond his reach. And yet she had

176

responded to his ardour with a fervency which stirred his blood. Why, then, had she turned away from him so suddenly, so violently? He could have sworn that the moment had meant as much to her, as to him, which made her sudden reaction even more inexplicable.

'Any more jobs for me, sir?' Wilkins asked.

David shook his head absently.

'Not just now, Wilkins. Report back for night duty at ten, will you?'

'Aye, aye, sir!'

When he was alone, David stood for a long time looking out to sea. The tropical evening was warm, with a dusky mist merging the horizon into the sky. The seas were calm and serene, in complete contrast with the state of his own mind, which was one of turmoil and confusion. Not for a long time had he been so emotionally disturbed, and it was Helen who was responsible. He could think of nothing, and no one, else. Even as he went about his work, examining each patient with meticulous care and thoroughness, a secret corner of his mind was still occupied by her alone. She had greater power to disturb him than any woman he had ever known.

It is because I love her, he thought with sudden clarity. I have always loved her—*will* always love her. And although she turned away from me so violently, I can't believe she doesn't feel the same. She couldn't have responded as she did if she hadn't felt exactly as I felt.

With the realisation, his heart lifted, soaring upwards on wings of hope. He loved her wholeheartedly, and if he couldn't have her, he wanted no other woman.

But I will have her, he resolved. I'll break through her reserve again, as I broke through it to-day. I'll do more than that. I'll love her and possess her.

I'll marry her.

CHAPTER NINETEEN

Throughout the night Lola was disturbed by her child's restlessness. Carol tossed and turned, muttering indistinguishably. The deep and distant throb of the ship's engines seemed to echo the anxious beating of Lola's own heart, offering no comfort, no assurance. She was frightened—frightened as she had never been before.

What can I do, what can I *do*? she thought in panic. Nothing but the things Helen had told her to do, the small attentions necessary to the child's comfort. At intervals Helen came to take Carol's temperature, feel her pulse, and administer an injection, but she had other patients to visit and for the most part Lola was left alone with her child.

She had a feeling of helpless inadequacy

which was frightening, the more so because she was unfamiliar with it. It undermined her self-confidence, of which she had always had an over-abundance. She could walk into a room crowded with famous people and not feel inferior. She could appear in public, supremely radiant. She could face a battery of cameras without flinching. And yet in the normal kind of crisis which might face any mother she was helpless and afraid.

She wanted someone to lean on, badly. Preferably a man. David was never around these days—he was too much in demand as ship's doctor. She tried to summon up a resentment against him and failed, aware that he was doing all he could possibly do and that other patients were entitled to his attention, but somehow, since he had stepped into Doctor Brent's shoes, she had lost touch with him. He had gone beyond her reach.

It doesn't matter, she assured herself. It will only be temporary. As soon as Paul Brent is back in harness, David will return to me. I've got to be patient, and, oh, God, how I *hate* being patient!

That was what Steve used to tell her, 'If only you'd have a little patience, darling . . .' He'd say it when she reproached him for being late, or when some household hitch occurred, or when Carol was naughty and she, her mother, just couldn't cope. 'Have patience,' he'd say, 'and everything will work out . . .' And

179

somehow it always did.

But he wasn't around to say it now. When married to him, the complacent words infuriated her, but right now she would have been glad to hear them. Instead, she was alone and there was no one to comfort her. She turned her face into her pillow and wept tears of self-pity.

Carol muttered indistinguishably and Lola sat up with a jerk. The child was rambling, and this terrified her mother. She couldn't understand how Sister Cooper could remain so calm about it all. Callous, that was what she was! Callous, as all nurses were! I hate her, Lola thought wretchedly, and if she cared two hoots about Carol she wouldn't leave me to cope alone, like this.

Oh, God, I'm tired! Tired and terrified! If Carol dies, what shall I do? I'll have nothing, and no one, to live for.

She hurried to her child's bedside. The little brow was hot and damp, the curls matted, the lips white. Helen had left a subdued light beside the bed, so that her mother could glance across the room and see if Carol was all right. For that, Lola supposed she should be grateful, but she would have been much more grateful for some capable person to nurse the child constantly.

She was kneeling beside Carol's bed when the door opened quietly and David entered. For a moment he stood watching Lola. She

180

looked like a crumpled doll, helpless and bereft—and anything but glamorous, he thought with secret commiseration, as he beheld her dishevelled hair and swollen eyes.

At the same time, he felt an impatience with her, as a doctor must always feel towards a mother who could only stand and weep.

He came across, placed a hand beneath her elbow and lifted her up. 'Don't get too close,' he advised practically, 'unless you want to take the infection yourself.'

'I don't care if I do!' Lola burst out passionately. 'If anything happens to Carol, I shall kill myself!'

Oddly enough, that didn't seem to disturb David in the least.

'You won't,' he said, 'because for one thing she isn't going to die and, for another, it wouldn't help if you did.'

'I've no one to live for but Carol,' Lola answered in mute misery, and this, David realised, was true. But he refrained from pointing out that it was her own fault, or that greater vigilance as a mother might have spared her child this illness and herself the anxiety.

'Have you slept?' he asked.

'Not a wink.'

'I'll prescribe something—'

'I won't take it! I want to stay awake, for Carol's sake.'

'Unless you get some sleep, you won't be

181

much use to her. And don't forget that the medical staff is keeping an eye on her. Helen is looking in regularly, I know.'

Lola gave a helpless shrug and drew a gossamer negligée around her. The night was hot and breathless. She leaned her head beside the open porthole, grateful for even a touch of tropical night air, and passed her hand wearily over her brow. It was a gesture she had used many times, with great effect, in dramatic moments upon the screen. This time she used it unconsciously and David's heart was touched.

He had a sudden instinct to make her talk, an awareness that it would help her to unburden her heart. For the first time since he had known her he felt that with one slight push the façade behind which she existed could be toppled over. And a good thing, too.

So he weighed right in by asking abruptly, 'What has happened to your husband? Where is he?'

'Steve?' She jerked round in surprise. 'I—I don't know. Why?'

'I just wondered.'

Suspicion and fear showed in her eyes.

'*Why?* Is Carol worse? Do you think he should be sent for?'

'Of course not. Carol isn't in the slightest danger—you've already been told that. The fever will run its course and by the time we reach Buenos Aires, if not before, she'll be

182

running about again. This epidemic is a nuisance, but not serious. You've been told that, too.'

She let out a long, slow sigh of relief.

'I'd like a cigarette,' she said, automatically holding out her hand with the gesture of a queen in command.

'Sorry—no smoking in a sickroom. Why don't you go on deck and have one there, if you really need it?'

'No—no—I won't leave Carol.'

She began to pace the room restlessly.

'Why haven't you visited her more often? Why do you leave it to Sister Cooper?' she demanded suddenly.

'Because after the doctor examines a patient the nurse takes over. And you couldn't find a better nurse than Sister Cooper anywhere.'

Lola's mouth curved in a bitter little smile.

'You always stick up for her, don't you?'

'Naturally. And so long as you attack her, I shall continue to.'

'Why?'

'Because I dislike injustice, and all your accusations against Helen are unjust, and you know it.'

Lola stood before him in an appealing and helpless attitude which would have gone down well with her public.

'David,' she whispered, 'are you angry with me?'

'I was—but not now. I feel sorry for you,

183

instead.'

'*Sorry* for me? Thank you! I want none of your pity.'

'I'm sorry for any mother of a sick child.'

'I see.'

So that was all she meant to him. Her feeling of inadequacy came flooding back. With his coming she had felt less alone, less bereft. She wanted to lean on him, not as a doctor but as a man, and instead he was merely concerned for her in a professional way.

'Do you ever hear from your husband?' he asked conversationally.

'Only through solicitors. Steve,' she said bitterly, 'is a very busy man . . .'

'As his wife is a very busy woman.'

'I am no longer his wife.'

'Sorry—I was forgetting.'

She began to pace the room again, talking in a whisper. 'He writes to Carol, of course. He adores her, in his way . . .'

'Then he must miss her.'

'I shouldn't think he has time to. He's either in London or New York or busy at his steel mills in the Midlands . . .'

'And right now?'

'New York, I believe. Not that I care. He could be in Timbuctoo as far as I am concerned.'

'But what about Carol? Doesn't she miss him?'

'Not in the slightest. She's forgotten him, I'm sure. Oh, she's glad enough to get his Christmas and birthday presents, his occasional letters, but in between she doesn't even mention him . . .'

David said nothing. Lola continued to pace the room restlessly, her thoughts roaming at a tangent, glad of release.

'Our marriage was a mess, an absolute mess. I was thankful when it ended.'

He didn't ask what turned it into a mess. He said nothing at all—just waited. Out of the mêlée of her words some distinguishable thread might emerge which would aid him in his quest to help Carol.

'Of course, it was his jealousy that did it. jealousy of me, of my career, of—'

'Of men?'

She shrugged.

'Can I help it if men fall in love with me?' When David made no answer she came and stood before him, smiling up at him wistfully. 'All men except you.'

He turned to Carol. The child was breathing more evenly; her mutterings had ceased.

'Go back to bed, Lola. Carol's going to be all right. Sister Cooper or myself will look in during the night . . .'

She felt rebuffed and a touch of her normal petulance crept into her voice again.

'Don't trouble. I'm perfectly capable of looking after my own child!'

185

'Are you? Then I'm glad to hear it.' His words were softened by his smile. Putting his hands upon her shoulders he said gently, 'My dear, why don't you cable your husband to fly down from New York—if he *is* in New York?'

'Oh, he is! I heard from Carl Brettard—he's his stockbroker on Wall Street. Carl acts for me still in a few deals, so from time to time I hear from him. But nothing would induce me to get in touch with Steve. He's gone out of my life for ever and as far as I am concerned, he can stay out.'

Her voice was emphatic. Too emphatic. David said nothing and departed.

Lola stared at the closed door, then flung herself on to the bed and burst into tears. *'Oh, God, I'm so lonely . . . so desperatety lonely! What's the use of living this way—unwanted and unloved?'*

Carol stirred, muttering in her sleep. Lola's tears ceased abruptly and in a flash she was beside the child. Laying her wet cheek against Carol's little hand she murmured, 'But I have got you . . . I have got you, my darling . . .' She clung to the child's fingers as if, in a failing world, they were all she had left to hold on to. Everyone else had let her down. Men especially.

Steve first, and now David. In some inexplicable fashion he had eluded her and all her bright hopes for the future now seemed as nebulous and insubstantial as a dream. And she was afraid.

186

CHAPTER TWENTY

An hour before docking at Salvador, Paul stirred and opened his eyes. Dimly, as if from a great distance, he saw a face—small and heart-shaped and indistinguishable—and in a remote corner of his consciousness he knew that it was pretty. He sighed, closed his eyes again, and slept.

Belita held her breath. His glance held comprehension, she was certain, for it had been unlike other moments when Paul stared unseeingly into space.

She had never realised, until her lonely vigils at his bedside, that a person could open their eyes wide and yet see nothing—persons other than the blind. It had frightened her, seeing Paul like that, but something in his very helplessness had deepened her girlish susceptibility into a more mature thing—the first awakening of an adult love.

After that brief glance the quality of his breathing seemed to change and when the door opened and Helen entered, Belita held up her hand with a new and touching air of authority. 'Ssh!' she whispered. 'I think he's sleeping.'

He was. Properly, this time. Helen was satisfied by his pulse rate and smiled her approval at Belita. 'You're a good nurse,' she

187

said. 'Your vigilance has helped him.'

Belita flushed. Somehow that word 'vigilance' seemed to imply more than Helen intended. It made the girl conscious, for the first time, that her devotion must have been very revealing to others. To Helen especially. And yet there was no touch of amused indulgence or pity in Helen's tone, so perhaps, after all, she had not guessed the truth. That was the last thing Belita wanted anyone to do, and particularly Helen, whose name had been linked with Paul's in shipboard gossip—gossip which, Belita suspected unhappily, was not unfounded.

Helen said kindly, 'Why don't you go up on deck and get some air? We're within sight of Salvador. People are crowding at the rails.'

'I've seen Salvador many times.'

'Of course. I forgot.'

Belita rose obediently, all the same. Not because she wanted to leave, but because she was suddenly self conscious and aware that an over-eagerness to remain with Paul would be embarrassingly significant.

Nevertheless, she couldn't resist one question.

'Is he going to be all right now?'

'Quite all right, Belita. The worst is past. You can go ashore and enjoy yourself—'

'But doesn't he need nursing any more?'

'He certainly does. Recovery will be slow because he's been very ill, but the medical staff can do all that is necessary.'

There seemed nothing more to say, but still Belita lingered, taking one last glance at Paul's sleeping figure.

'I think he knew me. At any rate, he knew someone was there . . .'

'That's a good sign,' smiled Helen.

She looked at the pretty young face and her heart smote her. 'You've been cooped up in here far too much, Belita. Doctor Henderson and I will have to be tough with you if you refuse to ease up now.'

'But I've enjoyed it! Nursing, I mean. At home, when my mother has one of her bad headaches, I am the only person she wants around.'

'I can understand that.' Helen looked at the girl's gentle face and thought how sweet she was and what a devoted little mother she would make, one day. A devoted wife, too.

Outside in the corridor Helen met David. 'How is Brent?' he asked.

'Showing signs of improvement—sleeping naturally for the first time. Belita says he recognised her just now.'

David glanced at Belita's retreating figure. Her slim ankles were disappearing up a companionway to the deck above. He smiled and said, 'Then I'm not surprised he's showing signs of improvement. To come out of a coma and see Belita's pretty young face would certainly do him good.'

189

Something in his tone brought an inquiring glance from Helen, but suddenly she didn't have to ask what he meant. She stood stock still.

'You mean that he and Belita—?'

'Are attracted by each other. And well suited, don't you agree?'

'I—I hadn't thought much about it—'

The surprise in her voice was so evident that David glanced at her questioningly.

'But everyone else has noticed it,' he said. 'You, too, I thought.'

'Oh, I knew Belita might have a sort of schoolgirl crush on him, but nothing more than that . . .'

'A great deal more than that, I suspect. And why not?'

When Helen didn't answer, David said easily, 'I think they'd be rather well suited, don't you?'

'I—I wouldn't know . . .'

She escaped to her cabin and, once alone, sat down weakly. She felt as if a door had opened, a door which she herself had been afraid to push lest, in so doing, she would hurt Paul. She had decided to shelve the problem until he was better, and now she wondered hopefully whether there was to be no problem after all. Paul and Belita, she thought wonderingly. Belita and Paul. Could David possibly be right about them?

As he said, why not?

A shaft of sunlight pierced the cabin, spilling through the porthole like a spotlight. Some of its brilliance seemed to enter her heart, filling it with light and hope. She wanted Paul to be happy—she wanted that sincerely— but she also wanted to find happiness herself, with David. Once she was free she need no longer evade the truth, no longer turn her back. She could go to him openly, hands outstretched . . .

But, first, she had to ask Paul for her freedom, and give him his. She had to make sure that he would be all right, and happy. That was the very least she could do, the least she owed him. Until then, there must be no more weak moments; if possible, she must avoid being alone with David, because if she were, desire might overcome both reason and conscience.

She could hear the vigorous hooting of tugs outside her porthole—and suddenly she was eager for her first glimpse of Salvador. The pilot had come aboard long since and very soon now the *Carrioca* would be skilfully docked. She hurried up on deck and joined a group at the rails. Their excitement was infectious and she felt herself carried forward on mounting anticipation.

But it was more than anticipation of her first glimpse of an alien and colourful port—it was anticipation of the future, a future which had been suddenly filled with hope.

Overhead an aeroplane zoomed, flying low. The roar of its engines drowned even the hooting of the busy little tugs. She glanced up, seeing the plane etched against the sky like a great silver bird. It was an American clipper— she could see the markings quite clearly. Suddenly she saw David standing nearby, shading his eyes against the sun as he followed the course of the plane.

She let her glance rest upon him, taking in the clear-cut lines of his face and admitting to herself, without reservation, that she loved him. She loved everything about him—his strength, his reserve, his intense masculinity. Suddenly the wonder of it seemed to overflow in her heart, recalling the touch of his lips upon her own. They had been passionate kisses, such as Paul's had never equalled.

The clipper disappeared over Salvador, heading towards a nearby airport, perhaps, for it was obviously in descent. A moment later it disappeared from sight and David dropped his hands. There was an expression of satisfaction upon his face which she could not understand.

He saw her then and came over. 'I'm going down to take a look at Carol,' he said.

'She's just the same. Condition unchanged. She hasn't improved as we expected her to . . .'

'All the same, I think she will,' he said confidently. He turned to go, hesitated, then came back. 'I don't suppose we'll have much chance to go ashore, but if we do, will you dine

192

with me, Helen?'

Her resolve not to be alone with him went whistling down the wind.

'I'd love to, David.'

He touched her hand.

'Good,' he said, and was gone.

Once the ship had docked and permits had been issued, passengers spilled ashore. Quite suddenly the decks were deserted, the lounges empty, the bars idle. The *Carrioca* was like an empty city, waiting for the invading hordes to return. Behind the scenes ship's personnel were busy, particularly in the purser's office, where the arrangement of accommodation for new passengers had to be carried out smoothly and swiftly. A large number of people left the ship at Salvador, to be replaced by other passengers en route for Buenos Aires. In twenty-four hours the ship would proceed, restocked and reorganised.

Throughout the quiet hum of activity Paul slept peacefully and Helen went about her duties with a light heart. Dinner with David . . . dinner in some quiet and intimate little restaurant, or some exciting and popular place which, to her, would be an adventure?

She knew which she wanted. In the old days David had always chosen the small and intimate places, and she wanted this trip ashore, if it came about, to be a replica of the old days—but more, much more besides.

Everything seemed propitious, everything

hopeful. She wasn't even worried about Paul any more, for in a secret corner of her mind she knew that Belita would be more than solace for him. It was only a question of patience, of biding her time, of waiting for him to get well again, and then telling him quite frankly that she wouldn't marry him, and why. He might take it badly, he might take it well. He might make a scene, or none at all. But however he took it, the truth had to be told, and in the end he would be grateful.

She wasn't really afraid—not any more. Her love for David strengthened her. She had even stopped fearing Lola's rivalry although it was obvious that the film star still clung to him.

No one could do anything with Lola but David. Murray Peterson lost his temper with her; Mike Saunders was out of patience. She wouldn't rehearse, or study her lines, or mix with any of the film company. She was temperamental and moody, wanting only her child and David. She would ring him at all hours, begging him to come to Carol, pleading for his reassurance, weeping hysterically into the phone. If Helen answered, she would hang up abruptly, or order her, peremptorily, to put David on the line.

And throughout it all David was patience itself, reassuring her, doing his best to assuage her anxiety. But he did it all as a doctor, with professional indulgence. As a nurse, Helen was too familiar with the pattern to mistake it for anything else.

Besides, could he have kissed her, Helen, in the way he had done, if another woman occupied his heart?

So it was in a mood of high hope that Helen went about her work—a mood of almost bemused enchantment. She was physically tired, worked off her feet, in constant demand, yet hope gave her a buoyancy, carrying her through the hours on light wings.

It was in such a mood that, in the course of her rounds, she passed through the lobby of the promenade deck—the main lobby by which first-class passengers came aboard—at the precise moment that a new passenger arrived. He came hurrying up the gangway, stepping briskly into the thickly carpeted foyer—a large man, wearing a well-tailored suit of tropical linen; brisk, businesslike affluent.

He wasn't handsome, but something about him—his air of success, perhaps—was arresting, but what caught Helen's attention was the fact that David was waiting to greet him, standing there by the sliding door which opened straight on to the covered gangway.

He didn't tell me he was expecting anyone, Helen thought remotely as she went on her way. Who was the newcomer? Some medical authority, perhaps, whom David had been delegated to meet. But he didn't look like a medical man—he looked too worldly, too rich.

195

Doctors rarely acquired an air of great material success; their work absorbed them too much, and work which concerned the humanities never left a moneyed stamp upon a person.

But she forgot the newcomer when she entered Paul's cabin. To her surprise, he was awake. His tired eyes revealed bewilderment and a kind of helpless disbelief, but a flicker of life showed in them when she entered.

'How long have I been here?' he asked weakly, and when she told him he stared aghast. She smiled and reached automatically for his pulse. 'You've had a bad time, Paul, but you're over it now. In a day or two we'll have you up on deck in the fresh air."

'We?' he echoed.

'Doctor Henderson and I.'

'Doctor—Henderson?' he repeated weakly.

'David Henderson—alias Keith Hennell, the author. He's a qualified doctor and stepped into the breach. So you can lie back and stop worrying about a thing. Everything is under control.'

His wrist turned within her fingers; his hand covered her own, clinging with desperate need.

'That sleep has made a new man of you, Paul—'

'You mean *you* have. I've been aware of you, dimly, all the time.'

She opened her mouth to speak, but he cut her short.

'It's all a bit hazy, but you've been here—I know. You've sat beside me and looked after me and I couldn't even say thank you—'

'Paul, it wasn't—'

'I know it wasn't any trouble to you—you're that kind of a person. That's why I love you. Oh, my darling, I can't tell you how I need you, want you, always . . .'

Something inside her went numb. His eyes looked at her with the patient devotion of a sick animal. And then he smiled.

'Gosh, but I'm hungry. And I could do with a shave.' He passed a shaking hand over the stubble on his chin. 'Six days growth at least,' he murmured with a wry grin. 'I must look like Convict 99 . . .'

She laughed a little shakily. 'No—you look just like yourself with a six-day growth . . .'

She thought frantically, I've got to tell him—soon—soon. But how soon? He was in no state yet to hear the truth. And it was her job, as a nurse, to spare him shock.

'I'll take your temperature,' she said, 'and then see about some light refreshment for you.'

'Light!' he protested. 'I need strengthening with some good roast beef of Old England.'

She placed the thermometer firmly in his mouth.

'A lightly boiled egg,' she said with professional pleasantry, 'and a glass of milk. That will be all right to start with, and after

197

that you will sleep again.'

He murmured an unintelligible protest. She removed the thermometer, took the reading, and ignored his indignant demands for a grilled steak. 'You're certainly better,' she said brightly. 'I'll send Wilkins in to give you a shave.'

'Helen—wait—'

She was at the door, but his pleading glance brought her back. He held out his hand to her and she took it with gentle compassion. He was pitifully weak and had lost weight—but that would come back. So, too, would his strength, and when it did she would tell him. Everything.

He closed his eyes with a tired sigh.

'Helen—'

'Yes, Paul?'

'I love you . . .'

She felt the prick of tears behind her eyelids and was glad he could not see them.

'I—I know, Paul—'

But love could change, couldn't it? If a young and pretty girl, a sweet and affectionate girl, came into his life and took possession of it, wouldn't it be possible for him to love her in an entirely different way? A way in which he would find happiness and enchantment just as she herself could with David?

His fingers tightened about her hand. He opened his eyes and looked at her.

'Helen, don't let's wait—to get married, I

mean. In the odd moments when my thoughts have been more or less coherent, one thing and one only has occupied my mind—the fact that I want to marry you, soon. I'm—sick of waiting—'

'Paul, you're tired—don't talk any more—'

'I must—'

'Not just now—wait until later—'

'No—I've made up my mind. When we finally dock at Buenos Aires I'm going to marry you, no matter what you say.' When she did not answer he whispered, 'Did you hear me, Helen? I said I'm going to marry you at the end of this trip and nothing, and no one, is going to stop me . . .'

She felt trapped. She stood there mutely, feeling his need for her binding her closely and relentlessly, for ever. And in a frightened corner of her mind a voice whispered, *It's too late . . . too late . . . you can't back out now . . . you can't back out now . . . It's you he wants, not Belita . . . you can't let him down . . . you can't, YOU CAN'T!*

CHAPTER TWENTY-ONE

By the time the *Carrioca* docked at Salvador, Lola had reached the stage where she refused to come out of her state-room at all. Carol's condition obsessed and terrified her. She refused to be parted from her child for five minutes.

The only person she would heed was David. At the same time she needed, and sought, Helen's care for her child. Agatha Armstrong was up and about again, but she was shaky and ineffective, goading Lola to fury. She would have none of her. Only one person should be allowed to nurse Carol, and that person was Sister Cooper. It was the duty of the ship's nurse, Lola declared, to accept responsibility for a patient who, but for her negligence, would never have been ill.

She was illogical and unreasonable, and to all her tirades Helen turned a deaf ear. She had met fractious mothers before, mothers who made scenes at the hospital, who had to be pacified even more than their ailing children. Mothers who wept. Mothers who hurled bitter accusations. They were in the minority, but unfortunately Lola belonged to that minority.

David handled her superbly. In his hands she was clay; she was as dependent upon him as a puppet upon its master. That was why he had no hesitation in taking a decisive step without consulting her. Produced as a *fait accompli* she could do nothing but accept it.

She was lunching when David tapped upon her state-room door—toying disinterestedly with a plate of untouched food. She had no appetite these days, not even for flattery and adulation, which had become meat and drink to her since becoming a successful screen star. She would have no one around her, except David—least of all members of the film unit. Mike Saunders said that if she went on like this she would flop in the best part of her career and she just didn't care. She wasn't so sure now that she wanted a career, anyway. All she wanted was to see Carol well again and to feel that she had someone like David to take care of them both. Then she could start life all over again, and a much better life it would be.

David, she felt, understood her as no man had ever done and the thought of spending her life with him was becoming a fixation. He handled Carol well, and the child would quickly accept him in place of her own father—Lola was quite sure about that. In between moments of panic over her child she persuaded herself that all would come right in the end—just as Steve used to predict—but this time it would be with a man far more suited to her temperament.

'I'm tired, that's what is wrong with me,' she assured herself as she stared unseeingly at her food. 'That's why I get frightened and imagine things—things like a change in David's attitude to me. He's a little brusque because he is busy, not because he's indifferent to me. No man has ever been indifferent to me. Not even Steve, when we parted.'

She jerked her mind away from that thought, refusing to remember the look of mute pain in his eyes, remembering only the angry line of his mouth and his grim refusal, at first, to give her up. But in the end he had surrendered, as he had always finally surrendered when she wanted her own way. And I dare say he's a great deal happier now he is free, she thought with unaccustomed generosity. At least he hasn't me to plague him. I suppose I did torment him a bit, from time to time . . .

Quite suddenly she wanted to cry. She cried a lot lately, uncontrollably and for no apparent reason. She knew that people were losing patience with her, irritated by a mother who resorted to hysteria when she should have been calm. But she couldn't help it. Carol was ill and she was alone, quite alone, and everything was getting on top of her. A few words with David now and then, reassuring as he was, were insufficient to lift her from the slough of despondency and self-pity into which she had sunk.

She put her head in her hands and let the tears flow unchecked. No one was likely to disturb her. David had looked in on Carol, and quickly departed. Too quickly. He had an appointment, he said, but he promised to be back. It wasn't time for Sister Cooper's visit and as for the Armstrong woman, she was keeping safely out of the way. So until Lola rang for her lunch to be cleared away, it was perfectly safe to unburden her heart in tears.

And it was at that precise moment that David knocked upon her door, opened it, and walked in.

Lola turned her head away quickly, conscious that she looked a sight. Her eyes were swollen and her nose was red. When she cried in a film the make-up man dropped glycerine tears in the right places, trembling beneath long lashes, lingering upon the curve of her cheek—enhancing, not impairing, her beauty. But this was the real thing—ugly and unbecoming, and she knew it.

The door closed, and he stood waiting. She mopped up ineffectively, saying with a shaky laugh, 'I'm afraid you've caught me at a wrong moment.'

'There's nothing wrong with it, except so far as Carol is concerned. In fact, I'm glad to see you so disturbed. But is it for the child, or yourself?'

For one brief moment she went rigid then, slowly, she turned. It wasn't David who stood there. It was Steve. He looked very large and capable and unyielding—the very qualities which she had once regarded in him as a sign of strength. Now they produced a welter of emotion within her—astonishment and relief, bewilderment and rebellion.

'How did you get here?' she asked stonily.

'I flew from New York as soon as I received

Doctor Henderson's cable.'

'*David* sent for you?'

'Is that his name? I only know him as Henderson. Seems a capable sort of fellow. Common-sensed, too. Traced Carl Brettard's address and wired me through him.'

Steve tossed his panama hat on to a chair and crossed to Carol, forgetting Lola altogether—or appearing to. Stooping over the child he whispered her name. There was no response. He tried again. Still no response.

'She's been like that ever since she was taken ill—and yet that ship's nurse insisted she would be well in no time!'

Steve took no notice. His broad back seemed implacable, dismissing her. He was concerned only about Carol. Tears of self-pity welled into Lola's eyes again.

'Doctor Henderson insists she is in no danger,' Steve said.

'Then why did he send for you? Why did you come?'

'Because he thought I could do the child good—that she needed me. I think so, too.'

Lola's self-pity gave way to anger.

'She has me!'

'You aren't enough,' he said candidly. He wasn't looking at her. He was sitting beside his daughter's bed, stroking her hot forehead in the old tender way. The gesture was so familiar that Lola could not bear to watch. It brought back too many memories. Once upon a time he had stroked her brow in much the same way, but not through anxiety. Through tenderness. Love.

In a mood of terrible frustration Lola declared bitterly, 'Well, the court thought I was enough—more than enough! *I* was awarded her custody, remember?'

'The courts make a lot of mistakes,' he replied frigidly. He wasn't angry, as he would once have been. He was merely cold—a stranger who appeared to have no interest in her. In a moment of rare honesty Lola thought: Well, why should he? We were all washed up, he and I, long ago. And after all, *I* am not interested in *him* . . .

Carol, who had been moving restlessly, was suddenly still. Her father looked down at her diminutive figure and his heart wrenched. Why had he been such a fool as to put up no fight for her? Why had he given her up so easily? Because, at the time, he was still in love with his wife and could deny her nothing . . .

For the first time he looked at Lola squarely. His face was impassive, but what he saw shocked him. Once upon a time her lovely limbs had been round and soft; now they were long and angular, beautiful from the point of view of a photographer, perhaps, but not from the point of view of an ordinary man. She looked older, too, and that had nothing to do with her present distress. There were lines about her eyes and mouth, lines of tension and irritability. So this was what success had done to her, he thought pityingly. And its devastation had not yet been completed. Ultimately she would become neurotic, overstrung, resorting to sleeping pills by night and tranquillisers by day, until at last her career petered into oblivion and she was tossed on to the scrapheap of yesterday's stars.

It was an ugly picture, but he saw it as clearly as if it had been painted upon the wall.

He said carefully, 'Carol needs more than one parent, Lola.'

'She will have more than one parent—and soon!' she flung back.

So she meant to marry again. Well, was he surprised? Hadn't he expected to hear of her remarriage long before this?

Covering his daughter's small hand with his own he said, 'I won't ask for the name of my successor. I'll only say this—that if you propose to replace me with a stepfather for Carol, I shall legally claim a greater share in her, and if I disapprove of the man I shall do more than that. I'll fight to get her back.'

She laughed. It was a mirthless laugh, but tinged with triumph.

'You'd lose. David will make an admirable substitute for you. He's fond of Carol and she of him and you said yourself, just now, that he was nice.'

Steve sat very still. So it was Henderson, the doctor, the man who had had the decency to send for him . . . In that case, Lola was right, he reasoned logically—David Henderson was a good type, a sound type. But not Lola's type.

'He'll never make you happy, nor you him.'

He broke off abruptly, for within his hand Carol's fingers had stirred gently. The childish mouth was moving, muttering inaudibly. He stooped closer.

In a flash Lola was beside him.

'What is she saying?'

Steve straightened up and looked at her.

'Just one word. Daddy.'

'I don't believe it!'

'Very well—listen.'

Lola knelt beside her child, taut with apprehension. She didn't believe it—she couldn't believe it. Why, Carol never even mentioned her father, never asked for him! It must be *me* she wants, she thought desperately. Mummy—that's what she's saying!

Suddenly the child sat up, opened her eyes in that, strange, unseeing stare which was so frightening, and called shrilly, 'Daddy! Daddy! DADDY!'

Steve gathered her up in his arms.

'I'm here, chick. I'm here.'

She was quiet at once.

Lola began to sob. 'I'll call David! He must come to her!'

'She doesn't need a doctor, Lola. Only me. And you later. You've got to be patient, my dear . . .'

Patience, he said, just as he used to. Calmly and reassuringly, lulling her panic.

Steve kissed his daughter's flushed face. 'I'm here, chick,' he whispered again. 'Daddy's here.' And after a moment the eyelashes fluttered; the eyes opened. This time there was no unseeing stare, but comprehension slowly emerging from a long way off, and on the childish mouth—the petulant, fretful, unhappy little mouth—a tremulous smile appeared. Then the eyes closed again and her breathing changed, becoming gradually more even, more relaxed, more deep.

After a while Steve straightened up.

'She'll be all right now. Doctor Henderson said that if only she could sleep naturally she'd come out of it all quite quickly. She was tensed up, he said. All tensed up inside. As a doctor, he seems to know what he's taking about.'

Lola made no answer. She was sitting slumped in a chair and there was something about her, an air of pitiful defeat, which touched her husband's heart.

'I'll be back,' he said, moving towards the door. I'm staying on board for the rest of the voyage.'

CHAPTER TWENTY-TWO

Helen and David were unable to dine ashore that night, but they snatched a brief hour off duty and spent it exploring the colourful vicinity of the waterfront. To Helen, it was all strange and exciting, but far more exciting was the fact that David was with her and, from time to time, put his hand beneath her elbow to guide her over unfamiliar cobblestones, or to protect her from the advances of waterfront characters with bold eyes and no scruples.

They lingered over drinks in a colourful bar, loitered in a narrow side street, where dusky children danced barefoot to the strum of a street musician's guitar, but beneath Helen's enjoyment lingered the memory of Paul's words, *'I'm going to marry you at the end of this trip and nothing, and no one, is going to stop me . . .'*

She thrust the memory aside, willing herself to live only in the moment—this moment. And it was a moment which ended all too soon, for at last the *Carrioca* was in sight again, looming up ahead of them like a vast floating hotel, and it was time to go back on board. Back on duty.

But before they did so David's hand found hers and held it. For a moment he felt a quivering response, and then she jerked away. Her reaction surprised him, for until now there had been no discordant note. They had laughed and talked together, as if there were no longer any barriers between them. Only once had he been disturbed by doubt, and that had been fleeting—so fleeting that he had persuaded himself it was imaginary. He had been looking down at her, remembering that moment in the surgery when their love had drawn them irresistibly together, and she, he was convinced, was remembering it, too. Then a shadow had flickered across her face, and he sensed a mental withdrawal which he could not understand. As if something, or someone, had come between them . . .

Now the abrupt withdrawal of her hand reminded him of the incident. It chilled him, and without another word he followed her up the gangway. At the head of it she turned to him, saying easily, 'Thank you, David—it's been fun!'

Fun. That was all.

He watched her descend a companionway towards the lower deck, and then walked thoughtfully to his own cabin. Once alone, he reviewed the past hour in his mind. They had talked of many things—of Carol, and her father, whom Helen had yet to meet; of Belita, who had retired to bed early instead of going ashore with a party to enjoy herself; even of St. Christopher's, very briefly. Once he had mentioned Paul, and she had replied that he was very much better and would soon be up and about again. Even back on duty, perhaps. 'And then you can return to the luxury life of a passenger, David!'

But he didn't want to, and said so. He had enjoyed these past days. But, of course, as soon as Paul Brent was ready to go back into harness he would have to step aside, and it would be Paul, not he, who worked once more beside Helen.

The thought depressed him. For the rest of the voyage he would be bored and frustrated, and not even writing would assuage that, for writing was a substitute in his life, a substitute for the career he really wanted. And it was then he acknowledged that ultimately he would, he *must*, return to medicine. Not only because Helen wanted him to, but because he himself wanted to. Medicine was his life. Writing about it could only be incidental, a contribution towards the whole.

Enjoyable as his walk with Helen had been, he was aware that in his heart he was disappointed. On the surface it had been gay and carefree, but now he acknowledged that there had been an element of guardedness in her attitude all along, and the reason for it eluded him.

As the days went by and the *Carrioca* continued on its voyage, David became more perceptive of Helen's moods, watching for that guardedness, that careful resistance which he hoped existed only in his imagination. It was not long before he was forced to admit that it did not. They worked together and talked together just as they did of old, friends and professional colleagues once more, but that was not what he wanted, nor, after those revealing moments in each other's arms, what he expected. She seemed to have erected a careful front over which he could not cross.

Rio, Santos and Montevideo came and went. There were parties, dances, and excursions ashore, and as the epidemic subsided rapidly after leaving Salvador, Helen had more time to join in. She did so whole-heartedly, enjoying every moment, but not once did she allow David to get really close to her again. She had made up her mind that until Paul was in a fit condition to be told the truth, she dare not let herself acknowledge the awareness which was ever increasing between herself and David; dare not let herself respond to him again.

Fortunately her duties kept her busy, even though she had fewer patients to attend. Carol's progress was rapid once her father came aboard; she no longer demanded Helen's attention, nor David's. So Helen had more spare time and took advantage of it. She bought gay clothes in Rio and wore them whenever possible. She swam a lot, danced in the evenings, played deck sports—but always with a party. Never alone with David.

Weakened by his illness, Paul's progress was

not rapid. He was content to do precisely as he was told, so long as Helen kept him company. She supervised his meals personally, sharing them whenever he begged her to. She sat beside him on deck when he was fit enough to be allowed up. She kept him constantly amused and interested, watching with a keen professional eye for the first sign which would tell her that he was becoming his normal self again; the first indication that he was well enough to face up to facts.

But long before that she told him about Belita.

'It was she, not I, who kept a watchful eye on you, Paul. I was rushed off my feet with other patients and goodness knows what I should have done without her help.'

To her surprise, he was not touched, but amused.

'Belita! That kid! What does she know about nursing?'

'Not a thing. She just did as she was told and appealed to me when necessary. For days you weren't fit to be left alone. She stayed beside you.'

'Bless the child! But I don't believe she'd have done it for anyone but you. She has the greatest admiration for you, Helen, she told me so.'

'Nonsense. Her concern was for you, Paul.'

But he didn't really believe that, Helen could tell. And there seemed no way to

213

convince him, especially when Belita herself denied it. 'Sister Cooper is exaggerating,' she said with a negligent shrug when Paul ventured to thank her. 'I did no more for you than for any other patient she asked me to help.'

'Then they were lucky, too. I hope you're making up for lost time now and enjoying yourself. I've noticed a lot of men on this ship queueing up for your attentions—it seems a shame to deprive them.' He patted her hand in a big-brotherly fashion. 'And don't forget to let me vet them for you. I promised to do that at the beginning of the voyage—remember?'

She said with a restraint which puzzled him, 'I am perfectly capable of looking after myself, thank you, Paul.'

'Hey! What's all this? Have you been growing up suddenly, or what?'

'I *am* grown up!' she said with a flash of temper. 'Please stop treating me like a child!' And to his surprise she turned upon her heel and stalked away.

He watched her departure thoughtfully. Seated in a sheltered corner of the boat deck, away from the blazing tropical sun, he was able to observe everyone who passed. There was a long sweep of deck before him and he watched Belita's swinging step as she hurried away. She was different, somehow. Not the shy little kid he'd felt sorry for when they set sail. In fact, as she said, not a child at all . . .

He felt an emotion which he was quite

unable to analyse. Being a practical man who liked straightforward situations and uncomplicated reactions he turned away from it. Belita was sweet. Pretty, too. Pretty as a picture. The man who got her would be very lucky. She'd marry young, of course, for her nature was warm and affectionate. He had a sudden picture of her as a radiantly happy young mother, with a bevy of dark-eyed children as lively and lovely as herself. For a man who was by no means imaginative the picture was a vivid one and it left him feeling oddly disturbed.

To his delight, and his relief, Helen appeared at that moment. She was wearing a gaily striped cotton skirt and sun-top and she pirouetted for his inspection. 'I hope you like the outfit,' she said. 'I bought it in Rio. The shops there were positively exotic. I wish you'd been fit enough to come ashore.'

'Wait until we reach Buenos Aires. We'll make up for lost time there.' But he didn't mean shopping trips, and well she knew it.

Dropping into a deck chair beside him she said, 'I'm off duty for an hour so I came up to have tea with you. I ordered it on my way. The deck steward should be along with it in a moment.'

Paul reached for her hand. She didn't resist him, but she didn't return his pressure. Instead, she lay back and closed her eyes. She could feel the warm tropical breeze fanning

215

her cheek and was grateful for it. It gave her the excuse to turn her face towards it, away from Paul. 'Whew!' she said. 'It is hot below decks now! This breeze is heaven-sent.'

'Turn this way, Helen—I want to kiss you.'

'Not in public,' she evaded lightly. 'Do you want to set tongues wagging?'

'They've been wagging throughout the voyage—surely you knew that?'

'I certainly did not! About us, do you mean?'

'Us, and others. Lola and Henderson, for instance. And they've been wagging even more since her husband came aboard. He's a nice chap, don't you think, despite his money?'

'Very nice. And Carol obviously adores him. She's becoming a different child . . .'

But she wasn't really thinking of Carol; she was thinking of Paul's remark. *'Us, and others . . . Lola and Henderson, for instance.'*

'What about Lola and David?' she asked abruptly.

'All sorts of things. That her husband's arrival has made no difference at all, except to Carol. You ought to know by now how active shipboard gossip can be. It has probably insinuated far more than the truth about you and me, for instance. Not that I mind. I'd like it to be true . . .'

'Well, *I* resent it!'

'But, darling, why? Let the tongues wag! Who cares? When we finally dock in a couple

216

of days the gossiping hordes will depart and forget all about us—and about each other. It's always the way. A pity, really. I would have liked them to know we finally married . . .'

'Here comes our tea,' Helen said thankfully, and busied herself with the tray which the deck steward set between them.

'And here comes Carol with her father. He spends hours with the kid, which is more than can be said of her mother.'

'Lola has improved, all the same. Haven't you noticed?'

'Can't say I have. She still seems nothing more than a walking clothes-horse to me.'

'That's unkind, Paul. Lola has a lot more to her than beauty.'

'True enough. She has a malicious tongue. D'you think the things she said about you haven't been repeated? Do you think I haven't heard them? Do you think I don't know that she blames the medical staff on this ship for a tiresome epidemic which might have happened anywhere in tropical regions? She wouldn't have created such a hullabaloo if her child hadn't been affected by it—and now look at the kid—she's got more colour in her cheeks and more light in her eye than when we set sail!'

That was perfectly true, and it was her father's doing entirely.

'Did you know that David cabled for her father?' Helen asked.

'I didn't, but it was a sensible thing to do. And very much in character, I'll admit.'

'You say that a little grudgingly.'

'Not really. I didn't take to him at first, but only because I had a ridiculous and quite unwarranted feeling that he liked you and you liked him.'

Helen placed two lumps of sugar in his tea, stirred it, and handed it to him carefully.

'I do like him, Paul. Very much.'

'As he likes you, I know. And I'm not jealous any more.'

She felt a sudden hysteria rising within her, for it was all so ironical. And 'like' was such an inadequate word for what she felt about David.

'Why aren't you jealous any more?' she asked.

'Because I know that's all there is to it—just liking. You've worked together since I was ill and there's nothing like work for reducing a situation between two people to its proper level—a sort of common denominator, if you know what I mean.'

'I don't think I do.'

Paul drank his tea appreciatively. 'This is good,' he said, 'and it tastes even better because you're here to have it with me.' He took another sip, then continued, 'I mean that working partners don't have time to get emotionally involved. Nor the inclination, usually.'

'You and I were working partners,' she pointed out.

'Ah, but we were much more than that before we came aboard. We were engaged even then, remember, and I only enticed you on to this ship so that we could be together— and *not* as working partners. It was to be a temporary arrangement, anyway. Still is. When we're married I'm starting as a G.P. back home. Life at sea is no life for a married man.'

She had a sudden impulse to blurt out the truth to him, to say, *'Paul, I can't marry you, and you've got to know why . . .'* The words trembled upon her tongue and in another minute they would have been uttered, but for the advent of Carol, who suddenly came racing towards them.

She hurled herself into Helen's lap, nearly upsetting the tea-tray as she did so.

'Whoa, young lady!' Paul cried. 'Do you want to spill tea down Helen's pretty skirt?'

Carol patted it admiringly. She looked, as Helen had said, a different child, a far happier child. Her father, big, solid and, as always, immaculately tailored in tropical suiting, came up behind and swung her high. She squealed her delight and for a moment Helen looked at them with undisguised pleasure. This was how a child should be with both parents—confident and unafraid and happy. Carol had never been that way with her mother, despite Lola's panic when she was ill. There was no doubt, after that, that Lola loved her child, but it was not a selfless devotion. Helen even had the suspicion that Lola's panic had been due to the terror of being alone, of having no one to love, no one who needed her.

If only she would go back to her husband, Helen thought, they would be far happier. Yet it was an open secret that Steve and Lola Montgomery had certainly not been reunited. Nor did they show any inclination to be. They were courteous with each other, friendly on the surface, and both spent a great deal of time with their child—in Steve's case, all his time. But Lola, once the crisis was past, had started rehearsing again and putting in an appearance in the Promenade Bar and the Veranda Grill and all the popular places aboard ship in which Mike Saunders liked his stars to be seen. She was back on her old footing with Murray Peterson—friendly enemies, once more—and again provided an exotic decoration each morning at the pool.

Nevertheless, there was a subtle change in her. She was quieter, steadier, more controlled. She drank less, too. It was as if a feeling of stability was creeping back into her life.

But if Helen hoped it was due to Steve's arrival, she was doomed to disappointment, for when on duty in the surgery next day, she had an unexpected visitor—Steve himself.

'I've been wanting to thank you, Sister, for

all you did for Carol. You've been wonderful to her—you, and David Henderson. The child has told me.'

Helen tried to wave aside his thanks, but he continued persistently, 'I could see I wasn't likely to get an opportunity to thank you before we dock to-morrow, so I came down to seek you out. Words are inadequate, I know, but Carol's happiness means a lot to me and I hope you'll accept this as a token of my gratitude—'

He held out a small parcel wrapped in the nautically patterned paper used by the ship's gift shop. When Helen opened it she caught her breath, for inside was an exquisite little Dresden figure—the kind she had admired often, but never been able to afford.

'Carol told me how much you loved them,' Steve Montgomery smiled. 'She said you gaze at them in the gift shop window every time you pass. It's a small thing, but it would make me happy if you'd accept it.'

'It will make *me* very happy to do so,' Helen assured him. She was very touched and looked at the big, affluent man with a new perception. Suddenly he seemed rather wistful and lonely, the kind of man who found it difficult to express himself and relied upon his money to do it for him.

She said frankly, 'Carol's recovery is entirely due to you, you know—not to either David or myself. She was fretting for you—David knew

221

that.'

'Yes, he has perception, I'll say that for him. So in the circumstances I shouldn't worry about him taking my place in her life, should I?'

Helen's heart gave a sickening lurch, then stood still.

'I—I don't understand—'

'It's perfectly simple. Doctor Henderson is to become Carol's stepfather and if it were any other man I'd fight like hell to get her back. As it is, I won't have to worry too much, for he is obviously fond of the child and understands her well. I'm sure he'll be equally understanding about my intention to see more of her, so perhaps the arrangement will work out satisfactorily, after all.'

Helen's mouth felt suddenly dry. She tried to speak, but could not. Steve Montgomery held out his hand.

'In case we don't get a chance to say good-bye before we dock, I'd like to say it now and to thank you again, Sister. I hope you'll keep in touch with Carol—she's devoted to you.'

At last Helen's voice returned.

'I'm sure she won't miss me so long as she is happy and loved—and I don't think Lola would want me to see her, anyway.'

'You mustn't worry about Lola, or take any notice of her petty accusations. Oh, I've heard all about them! She regretted them, too, once the child was out of danger. Lola has always lost her head in a crisis. She needs someone to lean on, always.'

'How well you know her, Mr. Montgomery.'

'I ought to. I was married to her for quite a time. I expect Doctor Henderson will understand her equally well.'

'You're sure of this?' Helen whispered. 'That they are going to marry, I mean?'

'Perfectly sure. Lola told me so herself. I've accepted the situation.'

And that is what I must do, Helen thought bleakly when she was alone. And more than that. I've got to forget that David ever took me in his arms, that he kissed me as if he loved me. I've got to forget everything about him, and the years in which I loved him. I've got to put all thought of him out of my mind and all longing for him out of my heart. But, dear God, how can I, when I love him so utterly and completely?

CHAPTER TWENTY-THREE

There was a general air of anticipation throughout the ship next morning, for Buenos Aires was in sight. There were elusive farewells, promises to keep in touch, much exchanging of addresses, and even a few sentimental tears.

'And within a few hours,' said Paul, 'they will

all have gone their individual ways, and forgotten one another. 'It's always the same, Helen—like the last day at school. Vows of eternal friendship and all that sort of thing. One or two will exchange a few letters, perhaps, or a card at Christmas, and after that the *Carrioca* will be forgotten. It's an unreal existence, this shipboard life—like sailing on the fringe of reality. Personally, I'm going to avoid all good-byes by hiding myself in a corner of the sports deck. It's sure to be deserted on the last morning.'

He was right. People were busy packing, or gossiping in the lounges, or having last get-togethers in the bars. No one felt in the mood for deck tennis or quoits. There was a sense of anti-climax in the air, as if waiting for the curtain to come down.

Paul settled contentedly with a book. He was feeling stronger every day, but Helen wouldn't hear of him lending a hand in the surgery. 'There's nothing to do but tidy up and check supplies, and Wilkins and I can do that. Every patient has been satisfactorily discharged, so you needn't think about coming back on duty until we're ready to sail home again.'

That suited him. He felt like a nice quiet morning in the fresh air. There was only one person to whom he particularly wanted to say good-bye and that was Belita Cortez, but she seemed to have no time for him these days. It hurt a little, because he genuinely liked the kid and had thought she liked him. But recently she never had more than the friendliest and most casual wave for him.

So much, he thought, for Helen's statement that Belita had been concerned for him when ill!

He had just settled himself comfortably when he heard a childish squeal and the thunder of running feet. Looking up, he saw a lively-looking boy chasing an equally lively small girl. It was the girl who squealed—with delight and spontaneous enjoyment. She could run, too—swiftly and well. The boy had quite a job to catch her. He was just within seizing distance when she saw Paul and pulled up abruptly.

It was Carol. Her face was flushed with pleasure and he could not help comparing her with the first time he saw her, yelling defiant rage at the unfortunate Miss Armstrong. Helen was right when she said that Carol was now a different child. Her smile was friendly, with no trace of defiance in it.

'Hallo!' she cried. 'I'm glad I've found you. Helen told me you were somewhere up on deck. I went to the surgery to say good-bye to her—and then I met Tony and forgot about you—'

Paul grinned.

'Well, that's honest, at least. And it was nice of you to think of me at all.' He held out his

225

hand and she shook it solemnly.

'You didn't get better as quickly as I did, did you?' she sympathised. 'Did you know you gave me the bug?'

'*I* did?' he echoed. 'And how, may I ask?'

'I was nursing you.' She giggled. 'At least, I was only pretending, of course, and Helen came in just when I was taking your temperature and rushed me into the surgery, and Uncle David stuck a needle into me, but it didn't do any good.'

'Well, I'm sorry I passed the bug on to you, Carol, but I can't say you look any the worse for it.'

'Nor does Belita. But then, she didn't catch it, which is funny, really, don't you think? Helen says she must have been immune, whatever that means. Anyway, it was lucky for her that she was, 'cos she looked after you all the time.'

'You're mistaken, young lady. Belita helped with many patients, that I know.'

Carol shook her head vigorously.

'Oh, no, she didn't! You ask Wilkins. He said she was your—your—' Carol frowned in a great effort of concentration. 'Your self-appointed nurse—that was it.'

Paul looked at her for a long moment, a puzzled little line between his brows.

'Wilkins said that, did he?' Then he finished briskly, 'Perhaps he made a mistake.'

'Oh, no. Wilkins *never* makes mistakes! He's

told me so, often.'

Paul laughed.

'I know Wilkins, young lady.'

That was true enough. The man was garrulous, but never a liar.

Suddenly Carol thrust a hand into her pocket and pulled something out. 'I've been meaning to give you this—I found it beside your bed that day. It's an awfully tiny hanky for a man to use. It can't be yours, can it, even though it has your initial on it?'

She held out a scrap of material. It was lace-edged and perfumed. He took it curiously and saw a delicately embroidered letter in one corner—the letter B.'

'It could be B for Brent, but *I* think it's B for Belita!' Carol piped. 'She probably dropped it one day when she was sitting with you . . .'

Suddenly she raced off in the wake of the boy Tony, leaving Paul staring at the handkerchief in his hand.

'I've come to say good-bye,' said a voice—a light, attractive voice with a broken accent. And there was Belita standing before him, dressed in an immaculate white linen suit with a scarlet handkerchief tied at the throat and scarlet sandals on her feet. She had an unerring sense of colour, for her lipstick and nail varnish matched exactly. But Paul saw none of these details. All he saw was her heart-shaped face and her large, dark eyes and the shy smile upon her lips.

He stood up instantly, aware of a sudden reluctance to let her go.

'We must have a farewell drink,' he said. 'I'll find the deck steward. Don't go away—'

She shook her head.

'I mustn't drink to-day—my father is meeting me and he wouldn't approve. And it would be useless for me to pretend—he would know!'

'He must cherish his daughter very much. I can understand that.'

A gentle flush touched her cheeks and her eyes fell. It was then that she saw the handkerchief in his hand.

'It is yours, isn't it?' he asked gently.

'Yes. Where did you get it?'

'It was found on the floor of my cabin, beside my bed. What made you say you didn't look after me, Belita?'

The flush deepened.

'I could have lost it in any other patient's cabin.'

'Don't spoil things, Belita. I'd like to think you were my self-appointed nurse.'

She didn't answer, but simply held out her hand.

'May I have that, please?'

'No,' he said, and thrust it into his pocket. 'I'm keeping it—as a souvenir.'

She looked up, and saw that he was smiling at her gently. Suddenly she said in a tiny choked voice, 'Good bye, Paul!' and stood upon tiptoe and kissed him. And then she was gone, leaving him with a breathless feeling in his heart.

He sat down slowly. There was no reason to be disturbed by the incident—it was a gesture, no more. A light and friendly gesture from an affectionate child.

But she wasn't a child—she had reminded him of that, angrily, only a short time ago. Nor was it the kiss of a child. And that was why it disturbed him.

He picked up his book, determined to read. He read three pages slowly and deliberately and didn't take in a word. He was thankful when he looked up and saw David Henderson coming towards him.

'I came to see how you were,' David said. 'Let's have a drink together before we finally dock—'

'I'd like that. We can have it here. The bars will be humming with effusive farewells.'

David summoned the deck steward and ordered drinks, then pulled up a deck chair and sat down. They chatted idly for a while, then Paul said, 'I've never thanked you for stepping into my shoes. You certainly helped us out of a tricky situation, and for that both Helen and I are grateful. By the way, I'd no idea you'd had medical training. What made you give it up?'

'An urge to write,' David answered lightly.

'Well, you've certainly been successful at it,

but you seem to be a damned good doctor, too. Helen thinks a lot of you, I can tell. In fact,' Paul finished with a grin, 'if I didn't trust her so much I'd be jealous!'

'Trust her?' David echoed.

'Of course. If a man can't trust the girl he's going to marry, it doesn't promise much for their future together, does it?'

David revealed no reaction whatsoever. He merely sat very still, very briefly, then said carefully, 'I didn't know you were engaged . . .'

'Before we ever came aboard!' Paul laughed. 'We kept it a secret. We thought it wiser. The Imperial Line frowns upon engagements between medical personnel, but to hell with that—we'll be married as soon as possible after we dock at Buenos Aires, I'm determined upon that. I've had enough of pretence.'

David finished his drink, laid down his glass, and held out his hand. 'Congratulations,' he said. 'I hope you'll be very happy.'

'Who wouldn't be, with a girl like Helen?'

'Who indeed?' David answered lightly, and went on his way.

Suddenly Paul called after him, 'Oh, by the way, good luck with the film!'

'Thanks,' David called over his shoulder, but he didn't look back. He went straight down to his cabin and shut the door. At any time of shock he preferred to be alone.

He sat for a long time, staring before him,

remembering moments when he had been certain that the happiness he had once shared with Helen had not only been recaptured, but had flowered into something more lasting and more lovely, and most poignant of all was that revealing moment in his arms. Her kisses, he had believed, were utterly sincere—as sincere as he believed herself to be. And all the time she was engaged to Paul Brent, who was lying ill in the adjoining cabin . . .

David's thoughts pulled up abruptly. So *that* was why she had jerked away from him— fleeing from him, he had said later, as if he were the devil incarnate . . . she had fled to Paul, because he had cried out and she had heard him. She had gone to him at once—he had found her in the man's cabin, a few minutes later. Well, at least she had a conscience, he thought bitterly. That much, at least, could be said for her.

Was it possible for a man to be so mistaken in a woman? Had the nurse he had known at St. Christopher's—the girl who had supported him so loyally at that fatal hearing—actually been insincere at the core of her? What else was he to believe now?

But Belita Cortez—what of her? Helen had not discouraged the girl's visits to Paul, even though it was painfully obvious to everyone that the poor child had fallen headlong in love with him. It only proved, he supposed, how certain she was of the man. She had reason to be, since she was secretly engaged to him.

David Henderson was not a passive man. When angered, his reaction was strong, and he was angry now. Angry with himself, for being fool enough to fall in love with her; angry with Helen for deluding him. Could life go on hurting a man for ever?

There was a tap upon his door. He opened it and there stood Helen.

'The captain asked me to find you. He'd like you to join him in his cabin for a farewell drink. He wants to thank you for your help . . .'

'No thanks are necessary,' David answered indifferently. 'I did what any other doctor would have done in the circumstances, and for no especial reason—but I'll go along to say good-bye. And while you're here I'll say good-bye to you, too. I hope you have a more pleasant voyage home.'

His voice was the voice of a stranger—utterly cold, quite impersonal. He shook her hand courteously, but the touch meant nothing at all. And then he was walking away from her down the corridor. Walking out of her life again. And this time, she knew, it was for good.

CHAPTER TWENTY-FOUR

Within an hour or two of docking at Buenos Aires the *Carrioca* was like a deserted city, with the crew as a remaining occupational force. Helen went ashore with Paul that evening, but could take little enjoyment in it.

'You're tired,' he said solicitously. 'It's been one helluva trip and what you want is a good night's rest.'

'An early night wouldn't hurt you, either. In fact, as your nurse, I order it.'

They were dining in a small restaurant in the heart of the city. Paul had planned to take her to the Splendide, the latest skyscraper hotel, but changed his mind on learning that Lola Montgomery and the film company had checked in there. 'It's the obvious place for them, of course. Like the Excelsior in Rome— "The place to go to be on show." '

'Are they all staying there?' Helen asked casually.

'So I understand from Uncle Joe. Their entire baggage had to be sent on.'

'David's, too?'

'I suppose so, since he is part of the outfit. I must say that surprises me. He never really seemed one of them.'

Helen replied crisply, 'Well, he's going to be permanently. He's going to marry Lola

233

Montgomery.'

Paul looked surprised.

'So the shipboard rumours were true? Funny—I never quite believed them. Not when I got to know the man. He turned out to be a first-rate doctor, didn't he?'

'Yes—first-rate.'

'I felt quite differently towards him after that.' Paul smiled at her a little sheepishly. 'Before I was ill I rather resented the fellow, you know.'

'I know.'

'I didn't like the way he used to look at you—a way I couldn't define. I realise now it was my imagination. Stupid of me.'

'Very stupid. And quite without reason. To him, I was never anything more than a competent nurse.'

'Never?' echoed Paul. 'I don't understand—'

Helen pulled herself up abruptly. At that moment she had been closer to revealing her early association with David than she had ever been, but she would never reveal it now. It belonged to the past, and if David himself didn't want it referred to, she owed him that much loyalty at least.

'I mean a competent ship's nurse,' she corrected.

They had reached the coffee stage and lingered over it pleasurably. A South American quartet beat out a seductive and insistent rhythm, and Paul said softly, 'Remember the night we dined at La Cucaracha—the night I asked you to marry me?'

'Of course.'

She felt a tight little knot of pain in her throat. Very soon she would have to tell him that she had changed her mind, that she couldn't go through with it, that she didn't love him enough, but she hadn't the heart to do so right now. This was his first taste of pleasure since his illness, and she couldn't spoil it.

It was also the first time he had been alone with her. Not even during the voyage had they been really alone, except for brief moments on surgery duty when Wilkins was on the wards.

She thought: If he talks about getting married here in Buenos Aires, I'll have to tell him, but until then I can let him be happy a little while longer. It is the least I can do.

So she changed the subject abruptly.

'Belita's father looked rather nice. Did you see him? He came aboard to greet her and was received with much ceremony. Uncle Joe tells me he's a prominent shareholder so it wasn't surprising.'

'I thought they lived in Mexico City.'

'Also in Buenos Aires. Pedro Cortez has vast interests here, including a hospital which he endowed quite recently.'

Paul said with swift interest, 'You don't mean the South American Foundation

235

Hospital just outside the city? It's a wonderful place, I hear. I'd like to see over it.'

'Then why don't you? You need only write to Belita and she would fix it with her father.'

'No—I wouldn't like to do that. It would be taking advantage of a shipboard acquaintance.'

Helen said with a smile, 'I don't think Belita would look at it that way.'

'Well, I would.' He signalled for his bill, closing the conversation.

Outside, the night was sultry. 'Let's walk for a while, shall we?' he said, taking her arm.

They strolled through the brilliantly-lit streets, rubbing shoulders with people of all colours and all races. Buenos Aires was cosmopolitan and stimulating—a new world superimposed upon a background of colourful history. 'We'll explore it to-morrow,' Paul promised. 'I'll show you all the sights, Helen. We have a week here before the ship is ready to turn round again . . .'

A whole week in which to arrange for their marriage—the implication was in his voice and in his words. And still Helen could say nothing. *Mañana, mañana,* she thought—isn't that what the Latin races say? And is their indolence infectious—or am I merely a coward, glad to postpone something unpleasant?

After a while they took a taxi back to the *Carrioca* and while they paused upon a crowded pavement, waiting for it to pick them up, Helen looked at a brilliant façade across the square and saw the word Splendide spelt out in electric lights. The whole place seemed elaborate and garish, not David's kind of place at all. And yet this was the world he had chosen, the life he wished to lead.

She was suddenly depressed, aware of a heartache which would not be lulled. Would it always haunt her? Would the memory of him torture her throughout her life?

The taxi whirled to a stop before them. Paul handed her in and, once inside, he kissed her. It was a warm and gentle kiss, but her heart went winging back to another moment, another man. David's kisses had stirred her as Paul's would never do.

She drew away gently. He said, 'Tired darling?'

'Yes—very tired.'

That was the truth, at least. She was tired in heart and mind and soul. Tired of loving a man who cared nothing for herself. Tired, also, of pretence.

'Paul—'

'Yes, Helen?'

She hesitated. A street lamp spilled its radiance through the taxi window, revealing his face in brief clarity. It was white and strained, the face of a man barely recovered from illness, and immediately her nurse's heart was touched. This was neither the time nor the place to distress him further. She had to wait.

She turned and looked through the rear window. The impressive façade of the Hotel Splendide was disappearing rapidly behind them—and David with it.

She thought desperately, 'I've got to forget him—I've got to! The sooner the ship gets me back to England the better. I'll sign off then and go back to St Christopher's, which is what I should have done in the first place.'

*   *   *

Paul rang Helen after breakfast next morning, saying that he wanted to talk to her. He added that it was important.

She knew what was coming and was reluctant to face it. She lingered over her bath, then donned a gay cotton dress she had bought in Rio and went to meet him on the boat deck. He had placed two chairs in a secluded corner.

He was looking more rested. He had had an excellent night, he said, and how about a cup of coffee? He had ordered that, too. A steward brought it just as Helen arrived. 'When he has gone, we can talk,' Paul said in an aside.

Unfortunately the steward was talkative, too, lingering as they drank their coffee, apparently impervious to Paul's thinly veiled hints. 'What I look forward to most,' said the man, 'is catching up on a bit of home news when we dock. Of course, the newspapers are a bit out of date, but better late than never.'

238

It was at that precise moment that they arrived—back numbers of overseas editions delivered to the ship in bundles. 'Ladies first,' said the steward amiably, handing the top one to Helen. Paul suppressed a sigh of irritation and said beneath his breath, 'Can't we send him off on some pretext or other? You know what I want to talk to you about, Helen—'

She murmured, 'Yes, Paul—I think I do,' and opened her newspaper deliberately.

But Paul was persistent. 'Then why are we wasting time? We've six more days in Buenos. A special licence won't take long to fix up.'

She glanced towards the steward, who was leaning against the ship's rail, deep in the news. Paul glared at him, casting about in his mind for some reason to dispatch him, but was jerked to attention by a smothered exclamation from Helen.

'What's the matter?' he asked, and turned to see her sitting rigid, as if something in the newspaper had startled her.

He glanced over her shoulder, but all he could see was a photograph of a little girl in ballet dress, and there was nothing about that to cause such a reaction.

The steward roused himself. 'Well, I'd better be on my way,' he said cheerfully, 'I've got jobs to do.'

'A pity he didn't remember them earlier,' grumbled Paul. He looked at Helen and said again, 'What's the matter, old girl?'

Helen didn't even hear him. She was reading the caption beneath the photograph, eagerly.

'Lovely little Christine Derwent, completely paralysed from the waist downwards three years ago, is now able to dance again. Experts predict a great future for her. See story on Page Five.'

Her hands trembled as she turned the pages—and there, staring at her with heart-rending familiarity, was David's picture, too. Her eyes raced down the newsprint. A whole column was devoted to the story, all of which was so painfully familiar to her that it seemed to have happened only yesterday.

Paul said with interest, 'Isn't that Henderson? What's he in the news for? Another book?'

'No, Paul—something far stranger, far more wonderful than fiction . . .'

Her voice was trembling, and her eyes were shining—shining with tears, he realised with a sense of shock.

'Helen—darling—what is it?'

She held out the newspaper, and he began to read about the child's early talent as a dancer, the tragedy of her illness, the hope of a cure, the final despair. Then he let out a low whistle.

'And it was Doctor Henderson who prescribed the drug? Poor devil—'

'Read on Paul. You haven't come to the end.'

He obeyed. The story revealed that the paralysis was only temporary, that after a few months Christine started to recover and, with the help of therapeutics, slowly regained the use of her limbs. A leading specialist was quoted as saying that Doctor David Henderson, in acting as he did, had actually saved the child's life, for although the injection caused temporary paralysis of the lower limbs, it prevented the germ from attacking her brain. And then came the photograph of David Henderson—'whom the child's parents would very much like to thank, if he could be traced.'

St. Christopher's Hospital, too, was anxious to contact him.

When he had finished, Paul looked at Helen for a long moment. Her tear-filled eyes did nothing to dim the sudden radiance about her.

'I *knew* he would be proved right, one day!' she whispered.

'You're in love with him, aren't you?' Paul said gently.

She nodded mutely. 'Yes, Paul—I've loved him for years. Please forgive me and understand, but I honestly thought—'

'—that the fondness you feel for me was love,' he said, a little sadly. 'I see that now. Why didn't you tell me you knew him at St. Christopher's? He was there before my time, I

241

take it?'

'All this happened shortly before you came. He resigned and went right away—no one knew where. I didn't tell you about him because there was really nothing to tell—there was nothing between us, you see, but a very dear friendship. At least, it was dear to me, but obviously it meant nothing to him. But all that is in the past. It was in the past long before I met him again on board this ship.'

'And you didn't say anything then because, obviously, it would have been disloyal to him.' Paul's kindly mouth tilted in an understanding smile. 'That is characteristic of you, Helen. You were sticking to me from a mistaken sense of loyalty, weren't you?'

'No, Paul—I was going to tell you the truth as soon as you were fit to take it. I almost told you last night, but hadn't the heart. I would have told you this morning. I came up here with the intention of doing so.'

He said evenly, 'If I were prepared to take you on your own terms, Helen, would you still marry me?'

'Loving another man? No, Paul, I couldn't. It wouldn't be fair to you—nor to myself, if it comes to that.'

'Even though he's marrying Lola Montgomery?'

'Even though.'

'Then what do you propose to do?'

'Go back to St. Christopher's. Matron said

242

there would always be an opening for me there.'

For a moment it seemed that he was going to protest or to plead. He opened his mouth, then closed it again deliberately.

Helen said urgently, 'I've got to find David, to show him this!'

'Of course.' Paul rose, and stood looking down at her for a brief moment, a sad little smile on his lips. Then he said practically, 'Would you like me to come with you?'

'No. It's not necessary. I'll put the cutting in an envelope and leave it for him at the reception desk at the Splendide.'

'Don't you want to show him the report yourself?'

'I'd like to, but he wouldn't want to see me. He was quite indifferent when he said goodbye.'

Paul said with sudden passion, 'I don't know how any man could be indifferent to you!'

Unexpectedly, she answered, 'But aren't *you* indifferent to Belita? Poor child—she's in much the same situation as myself . . .'

*   *   *

The lobby of the Splendide was as ornate as its exterior, with quantities of vast gilt-framed mirrors and gigantic chandeliers. People of all colours and nationalities passed Helen in a bewildering tide. She fought her way through them to the reception office.

At length a dark skinned and impeccably tailored young man bowed before her. She held out the envelope, saying, 'Will you see that Doctor Henderson receives this immediately?'

The young man echoed politely, 'Doctor Henderson? I do not think we have anyone of that name registered here.'

'Oh, but he came with—'

A child's clear voice suddenly piped, *'Helen! HELEN!'* and a moment later Carol flung herself upon her. 'I knew you'd come to see me!' she cried. 'I *told* Mummy so, but she said we'd have to get in touch with you ourselves when I asked and when *she* said—'

A man's voice cut across her excited chatter.

'Sister Cooper—this is a pleasant surprise! This daughter of mine never stops talking about you—'

And there was Carol's father, as large and prosperous as ever, but now subtly changed. There was an air of quiet contentment about him which was quite at variance with his earlier impression of impatient drive.

He shook her hand warmly.

'My wife and I intended to telephone the ship to-day, to see if you would dine with us this evening. Here's Lola now—she can issue the invitation in person.'

To Helen's surprise, he turned and beamed upon Lola, who stood still for a moment, a

244

flush of embarrassment flooding her face.
Helen's smile put her at ease, however, and
she came forward, saying, 'I'm glad you've
come, Helen. I owe you an apology and Steve
says I must make it. And since I always did as
he told me, once upon a time, I suppose I'd
better start doing so again.'

Helen looked from one to the other
inquiringly. There was something about them,
something in the atmosphere.

Steve gave a wide smile.

'Congratulate me, Sister Cooper—I've
wooed and won her all over again.'

Carol gave an excited little skip and jump.
She looked a different child.

'And we're going home for ever'n'ever!'

Helen's heart performed a sudden *allez-oop*,
then righted itself. She looked at Lola's
beautiful face and saw a quality of happiness
which had never been there before—the
happiness of a woman who suddenly found
herself secure and at peace.

'I'm glad—so glad!' Helen said, and reached
forward impulsively to kiss Lola's cheek. Then
she looked down at the envelope in her hand
and said, 'Would you do something for me?
Give this to David as soon as possible—it's
important.'

'David? But he isn't here. He took one look
at the Splendide and said it wasn't the place
for him. Too ostentatious. So he simply
collected his bags and walked out. Where to,

245

we don't know. Nobody knows.'

CHAPTER TWENTY-FIVE

Paul met Helen at the head of the gangway. There was something about her walk which told him the truth.

'You didn't find him.'

She shook her head mutely.

'No. He'd gone—moved elsewhere.' A tiny smile flickered at the corner of her mouth. 'Somehow I couldn't imagine him at a place like the Splendide.'

'But what about Lola? Doesn't she know where he is?'

'No one knows.'

He gave her a brief and discerning glance. 'What you need is a drink, old girl. We'll have it in state in the M.O.'s office and consider what's to be done.'

The drink did her good. She smiled at him and said, 'Well, at least I learned one good thing—that Lola has gone back to her husband.'

'That doesn't surprise me. I saw it coming before they left the *Carrioca*. She was putting up an awful lot of resistance, but I thought he'd win in the end. And I never did believe the tale about her marrying David. He was interested in her child because he has never stopped being a conscientious children's doctor, but he was never interested in the child's mother.' Paul finished gently, 'So now he is free to marry you . . .'

'He doesn't want to marry me. He has never wanted to marry me. I've accepted that fact, so don't let's talk about it.'

'All right,' Paul agreed briskly. 'But we've got to get that newspaper cutting to him somehow and we'll do it if we have to visit every hotel in Buenos Aires.'

'Which means, judging by the number, that the *Carrioca* will sail without us!' Helen put out a hand and touched his sleeve. 'Why are you so kind to me, Paul? Few men would be in the circumstances.'

He answered gruffly, 'Rot! I don't like to see a fellow doctor in trouble, that's all. But that isn't the only reason. I told him we were going to be married in Buenos Aires . . . which was probably why he said good-bye to you so coldly. The least I can do is help to put matters right.'

Helen sat quite still, aware of a sudden hope in her heart, until a tap upon the door brought her back to reality.

It was Uncle Joe, the purser.

'So here you, are, Doc—I've been looking for you. A call came through five minutes ago. I didn't imagine for one moment you'd be in your office at this time of day, so I took a message.'

247

'Yes?' said Paul absently.

'It was from Henderson—the man who stepped into your shoes on the way over—'

'Henderson!' Paul echoed sharply. 'What did he say?'

'Simply that he thought you might like to visit the new Foundation Hospital with him— seems to think it well worth seeing. Apparently he ran into the lovely Belita and her father just as he was stepping into a taxi outside the Splendide, and Cortez pressed the invitation upon him. If you're interested, he wants you to pick him up at his hotel.'

'*What hotel?*' Paul and Helen demanded in unison.

Uncle Joe regarded them in surprise.

'The Universale—never heard of the place, myself. Says it's off the Square Nationale. Anyway, a taxi driver will know it . . . Hey! What's the hurry?'

But the only answer he got was the echo of their footsteps hurrying along the deck outside. Curiously, Uncle Joe crossed to the ship's rail. A moment later he saw Paul and Helen hurrying down the gangway and along the dockside, frantically signalling for a taxi.

The purser scratched his grey head. He couldn't see what all the hurry was about. And anyway, Doctor Henderson had said three o'clock—but he hadn't had a chance to get that far.

*　　　*　　　*

The Universale was small, comfortable, and quiet. It offered David precisely what he sought— peace in which to write. He had a room at the back overlooking a quiet garden and everything was exactly as he wanted it to be.

And yet he couldn't write. A litter of discarded paper testified to that. He had torn up every attempt and now sat staring at a blank sheet of paper in his typewriter, waiting for the words to come.

After a while he rose and began to pace the room restlessly. His enthusiasm had gone—he had to face that fact squarely and resolve how to overcome it. But how did one reawaken an enthusiasm which had died? And why had it died? Because something in his own heart had gone? Hope? Determination? Love?

He wasn't a man who shirked issues and he didn't shirk this one. There were only two things he really wanted now—to return to medicine, and to have Helen. Well, he couldn't have Helen, but at least he could become a doctor again.

With the thought came sudden resolution. He would go back . . . back to England . . . back to St. Christopher's. The Super had impressed upon him, at the time of his resignation, that the board didn't want him to go and that if he ever wanted to return, he

249

could.

And he would. Even though the hospital wouldn't be the same place without Helen. Even though he would remember her every time he entered the children's ward. She would marry young Doctor Brent and be happy with him and in time the bitterness would leave his own heart.

The thought of Paul Brent pulled him up with a jerk. Why had he insisted upon including him in the invitation to the Foundation Hospital? Because there had been something in Belita's voice as she said, 'Perhaps Doctor Henderson's colleague would care to come, too, Papa—the other ship's doctor, I mean.' And David had known how badly she wanted it and had said the very words she wanted him to say.

'May I telephone him, Señor? He's a keen young doctor. I'm sure he would enjoy the visit.'

There was a knock upon his door. He called, 'Come in!' absently, and was surprised when Paul entered.

'You're early! I said three o'clock. The Cortez car will pick us up at that time.'

'Then I'll wait downstairs. Meanwhile, Helen has something to show you . . .' He drew her into the room as he finished, 'And *I* have something to tell you. We're not being married, as I said. Helen doesn't love me. She can tell you why.'

250

The door closed behind him.

David and Helen stood looking at one another, then he said stiffly, 'Won't you sit down?'

The stilted formality of his words made something snap inside Helen. She burst out furiously, 'Don't be so *polite,* David! Just take a look at this, and then I'll go.'

She held out the cutting. When he had finished reading it he realised that her hand was upon his sleeve and, swiftly, he covered it with his own. And then she was in his arms, his lips against her hair. They clung together, saying nothing, for words were superfluous. The world had suddenly righted itself, leaving no room for doubts or misunderstandings.

After a long moment he said, 'Marry me, Helen—marry me soon. I've waited so long—too long.'

'So have I, David.'

'I'll go back to St. Christopher's. I'll continue where I left off. And I'll work as I have never worked before because I'll have you to come home to. That's where I want you to be, Helen, at the heart of my life . . .'

*　　　*　　　*

Downstairs in the quiet hotel lounge Paul waited. He felt curiously at peace—not bitter in the least. He wanted Helen to be happy—she deserved to be. And one glance at David

251

Henderson's face as she entered his room had told Paul that he and he alone was the man for her, and she the one woman in the world for him.

As for himself—well, life went on. And he was young. And he wasn't the first man not to marry the girl he wanted—and to find, when it happened, that the hurt didn't go so deeply as expected.

He even had a sense of anticipation, as if awaiting a new chapter in his life.

And right at that moment it began. The swing doors from the street spun upon their hinges and a slim young figure entered—and stood still at the sight of him.

It was Belita, looking enchanting in a simple white dress, against which her olive skin glowed like amber.

He rose swiftly and went to meet her, aware of a sudden lightness in his heart.

'I hoped you would come,' she whispered. 'I hoped so much that you would come!'

Their hands met, and clung.

'It was selfish of me, wasn't it, Paul?'

'Why, selfish?'

'Because I didn't include Helen in the invitation. But it isn't too late, if you would like her to come along . . .'

'I don't think she'll want to come along. Nor David Henderson. They are upstairs very much absorbed in one another, I imagine. Need we disturb them?'

Her eyes lit up like twin stars.

'Not if you don't want to, Paul—but I thought, everyone thought, that you were in love with her . . .'

'I was once upon a time. But that chapter of my life is over, Belita. Shall we go?'

Hand in hand they walked out into the sunshine.